9/22

FLIP
TURNS

Catherine Arguelles

FLIP TURNS

Catherine Arguelles

JOLLY
FiSH
PRESS
Mendota Heights, Minnesota

First Edition
First Printing, 2022

Book design by Sarah Taplin
Cover design by Sarah Taplin
Cover illustration by Carl Pearce (Beehive Illustration)
Chapter icons by Shutterstock Images

Jolly Fish Press, an imprint of North Star Editions, Inc.

Library of Congress Cataloging-in-Publication Data (pending)
978-1-63163-635-6 (paperback)

Jolly Fish Press
North Star Editions, Inc.
2297 Waters Drive
Mendota Heights, MN 55120
www.jollyfishpress.com

Printed in the United States of America

for Isabel and Lillian:
you are the best things

Chapter 1

As my teammates jump into the pool for afternoon practice, I duck my head under the water to run through my flip turn for the millionth time.

I remember to center myself on that black line on the bottom of the pool and stretch my arms long, like I've been told. On my last stroke before reaching the wall, I fold at the waist, tuck my knees into my chest, and snap my toes over my head.

Planting my feet on the wall, I push off hard to swim a new lap. Halfway down the pool, I pop my head out of the water.

"That was good, right? Good enough that we can stop doing these now?" I holler at my best friend, Ez, in the next lane.

We have five minutes until practice officially starts, and I'm hoping to use at least four of them to tell her all about what happened after school today—our last day of seventh grade.

"That was awesome! Now watch me!" Ez yells. I take a breaststroke kick and glide to the wall so I can watch her flip turn. Ez speeds down the lane in her powerful freestyle. Her turn is so quick she sprays water all over my goggles.

When she reappears mid-pool, I give her a thumbs-up. "Amazing, as always."

Ez takes two giant strokes to reach me. She leans on the lane line between us and lowers her voice. "Okay. Spill. What happened today after school? With Lucas and the snow globe? You didn't chicken out, did you?"

I glance around to make sure no one is listening, then lean over to tell Ez, "I gave it back, like you and I talked about. And it didn't go well."

"Uh-oh. Tell me everything," Ez whispers.

I've been telling Ez everything since we started swimming on this team as 6-and-unders, and "every-thing" mostly means who I have a crush on. But for the last year and a half, it's meant telling her about Lucas Bryce and his big gross crush on me.

I tell Ez when Lucas messages me on Instagram wanting to talk about his family drama, or his feelings for me, or his love for hot dogs. I tell her how he keeps asking me out even though I always say no.

And last week, on my thirteenth birthday, one week before summer, I showed Ez the present Lucas had given me that day: a glittery heart-shaped snow globe sprin-kling heart-shaped snow on two tiny hugging polar bears.

Now I get to tell Ez the latest chapter in the Lucas Bryce unfortunate, uncomfortable, unwanted crush story. Ez bobs on the lane line with anticipation.

"So, I just put it in a paper lunch bag and handed it to him," I tell her. I can still picture Lucas standing in front of the lockers, a flop of chlorine-bleached hair in his eyes, T-shirt stretched out across his slumped shoulders. "I said, 'Sorry, but I don't think it's right for me to keep this. I don't like you that way,' and I just gave it back."

Ez's eyes widen. "Good job, Mad. What did he say?"

"He said, 'Okay, Maddie, so you don't like me that way, but you *do* like me?'"

"He did not!" Ez smacks the water, sending a splash onto the pool deck. "Tell me you said no."

"I just wanted to leave." I sigh. "So, I said, 'As friends. That's it.'"

"Uh-oh. Friend zone. He is gonna hate that." Ez shakes her head.

"Yeah. He tried to laugh, but it wasn't a real laugh. His eyes got like, all dark and weird, and when he walked away, he tried to be cool about it, but he was actually stomping his feet like a little kid."

"Ugh, so dramatic. But you did the right thing. He can't go on thinking he's got a chance with you when he doesn't."

"I know, I mean, he shouldn't have even given that to me. It's something a guy would give his girlfriend when they're, like, in high school, right? Or maybe never, because really who wants a snow globe?" I cringe. "I don't even like snow."

"Or polar bears!" Ez points out.

"Exactly! Every time I had to get something out

of the drawer where I put it, I wanted to throw up." I shudder.

"Well, now it's gone forever. And we can have a fun summer and not worry about Lucas." Ez grins.

"Uh, actually, it's not exactly gone. I saw it later, the snow globe." I lower my voice. "Smashed all over the sidewalk outside of school."

"No way! I knew I should have gone with you to give it back." Ez bounces up and down in the pool, creating a tidal wave that rocks the lane lines.

"It's okay. I thought it would be easier for him if there weren't other people around. But yeah, I probably should have had backup. It was creepy. I didn't see him smash it, so I don't know if he smashed it because he was mad or if he smashed it because he wanted me to see that he was mad." I pull the edges of my swim cap over the straggling ends of my wavy brown hair. "Or maybe he just, like, dropped it on accident."

Ez runs a hand over her head. She doesn't wear a cap because she was diagnosed with alopecia totalis in fifth grade and has no hair. She doesn't even have eyebrows. "I don't think it was an accident. I bet he smashed it because he was mad, and he did it where he knew you would see it."

The thought makes my stomach turn over. "Yeah. Maybe. I blocked him on Instagram. I don't want to see his posts anymore or get his messages."

"Good! Maybe he'll finally take no for an answer," Ez says.

"Let's hope so. I'm just glad he doesn't swim on our team, and his team only swims against ours once this summer." I stretch my arms over my head.

"Did you tell your parents?" Ez whispers.

I duck my head since my brother and sister are nearby. "Nope. They would just worry about my anxiety and think I can't handle it."

"But . . ."

Ez's protest is cut off by a high-pitched voice from the lane next to us. "Ezzzzzziiiee, I thought we were racing?"

Ez loves challenging Charlotte to a race before practice. The two of them have been locked in an ongoing battle for fastest East Valley Eel since we were in the 9–10s. Charlotte hasn't been wanting to race as much lately though, since we got into the 13–14 age group. I think she's trying to look cool for the older kids.

But her competitive spirit is on today.

"You get lane three, I get lane four?" Charlotte suggests to Ez. Lanes three and four are right in the middle of the pool and reserved for the fastest swimmers. The slowest swimmers are in lanes one and six on the ends. I usually swim in lane five.

"Yeah! Let's race—one lap! We've got thirty seconds before practice starts, and I can beat you in less than fifteen." Ez's red-rimmed eyes gleam. "Maddie, race with us?"

"No way!" It feels good to laugh after all the talk about Lucas and broken snow globes. "I am not getting in the middle of you and Char and your never-ending quest for ultimate glory."

"Hold up, speed demons! No racing yet!" Lexi hollers from the side of the pool, swinging her coach's whistle. "Practice first, then race. I know you're all just bursting with summer excitement, but we have a meet next weekend and that means we have work to do. Two hundred–free warm-up, let's go!"

Lexi crouches next to me while I adjust my goggles again. "That means you, too, little sis."

I roll my eyes. Lexi is nineteen and home from her first year at college. I fix my goggle strap around my ears. "Whatever you say, Coach."

"That's what I like to hear." Lexi pats my shoulder, and I push off the wall to join the rest of the 13–14 and 15–18 age groups.

All through the warm-up, Ez and Charlotte tease each other about who's going to win their little race. At the end of a grueling set of 50-yard sprints every fifty-five seconds where Ez comes in a half second before Charlotte every time, Ez gets a sly grin on her face and says, "Sure you want to race? Maybe you should shave your head first, 'cause I've got this streamlined advantage and all."

Charlotte tucks a stray blond hair under her cap and rolls her eyes. "Yeah, yeah. Like I haven't heard that one before." She eyes the blocks.

Ez lightly punches Charlotte's arm. "Or should we

record this for your famous TikTok account? Give you some exciting content."

"Now, that is a good idea." Charlotte spins in the water with dramatic flourish.

It's not even halfway through practice, but Lexi blows her whistle to signal a break.

"All right, you two, let's get this over with. Team!" Lexi uses her loudest coach-voice. "We're doing a 25-free fun race to honor the beginning of summer! Starting on the blocks: Esmeralda, take lane three. Charlotte, lane four. Who else wants to race with them?"

"Me! I do!" a couple of the boys from the 13–14s holler.

"Fabulous." Lexi snickers. "I love seeing you guys get beat by girls. Owen, take lane two. Aidan, lane five." Owen Wu and Aidan James live in the neighborhood, and we've been swimming with them for as long as I can remember.

Ez whoops. "You're on, dudes!"

Aidan gives her a friendly fist bump as they swim under the lane lines to the edge of the pool.

Lexi scans the water like a shark searching for prey. "All right, let's get a couple more of you 13–14s to round out the lanes. Sophie, lane six. Maddie, lane one."

"What? No!" I stick my face in the water and blow out some angry bubbles. Lexi said no special favors just because we're related, but she knows I don't like the kind of attention that comes from racing against our best swimmers.

I pop my head out of the water as Ez glides to me. "C'mon, Mad, let's do this. You can totally beat Aidan."

I rub water droplets off my goggles. "I don't think I can beat Aidan; he's grown like a foot since last summer." But protesting my part in the race would just draw more attention to me. "Fine." I smile at my best friend. "Let's do this."

Ez and I climb out of our lanes and line up with our teammates behind the blocks. It's late in the day, and the summer sun beats on our wet shoulders. The rest of our teammates gather at the sides of the pool to watch. A couple of girls from the 15–18s holler encouragement.

As I approach lane one, something catches the sunlight at the base of the block. I crouch next to the lane-one block and peer closely at the shiny object. My heart suddenly pounds. Is that glass?

Oh no.

My heart sinks deeper than it did when Lexi told me to do this race. If I had taken one more step, my toes would resemble a crime scene. But that's not what scares me.

I would rather see a piranha in the deep end than glass anywhere near this pool. Glass on the pool deck is like the dark cloud of the apocalypse; the potential for injuries with this many barefoot kids is unthinkable. I carefully pick up the two large shards and turn to Lexi.

Lexi's mouth drops open. "Maddie! What are you holding? Tell me that's not glass."

I'm sure Lexi, like probably everyone in the pool,

remembers the meet at River Oaks a few years ago where one of our 6-and-unders cut her foot on glass. There was blood everywhere. River Oaks had to forfeit the meet and give us the win.

Then the girl's parents sued the River Oaks club because the glass cut her tendon and the hospital bills were astronomical. River Oaks had to forfeit the whole rest of the season. That's what really scares me—an accident that would make us lose our season and our swim team. My heart races just thinking about it.

"Yeah, it is," I squeak. "It looks like a broken bottle or something."

"Where did you find it?" Lexi panic-screams. "How many pieces? How did that get here?" She grabs a pair of red flip-flops from the lifeguard box and hurries to my side.

"Under the block and, uh, I don't know?" I look around for more glass, but I don't see any. "I think it's just these two pieces." I shrug, but for a second, Lexi looks like she might cry.

Lexi takes a deep breath. "I'm sorry, I'm freaking out. Don't worry. Here, put these on and just, um, just sit on a block for a sec. Don't put your feet on the deck." Lexi blows her whistle. "Everyone! Stay exactly where you are! Do not move." She grabs her phone from a bench and touches it once before putting it to her ear. I'm pretty sure she's calling our parents, who own the East Valley Athletic Club and run this swim team.

There are all kinds of pool safety procedures that

have to be followed when something like this happens. I hope Lexi isn't too upset to remember them right now.

Ez and the other racers perch on their blocks, frozen in place while Lexi makes her call. No one says a word.

After a few minutes, Lexi puts her phone down and takes a deep breath. "All right, team. Here's what we're going to do. First, practice is canceled for the rest of today."

Usually that information would be met with cheers, but no one in this group would admit to being happy right now. I stare at the sign over the blocks that has a picture of a bottle with a red circle and a line through it and says in bold letters NO GLASS. There are at least six signs like that around the club. Right next to the ones that say NO RUNNING. Basic pool rules.

"So, should we get off the blocks then?" Aidan asks gently.

Lexi snaps to attention. "*No!* Not yet. There could be glass anywhere. Or everywhere. Don't move. I said that already. Don't move! I'm going to check the locker rooms, then I'll bring all of you your flops. You'll have to walk reeeealllly slowly to the locker room to get your stuff. Watch for glass every second." Lexi runs into the locker rooms while we all stare at each other in nervous silence, then she grabs the shoes lined up on the deck.

After we follow her orders, everyone hurries to get out of the pool area. We technically have almost forty-five minutes of practice left, so some kids text their parents and wait in the front to get picked up. But most of us live close enough to walk or bike.

As Charlotte leaves, she grabs Lexi. "Everything's okay, right? No one got hurt? Sorry that we wanted to race so bad."

Lexi sighs. "Oh, it's not your fault. And no, no one got hurt, but we'll have to check to see if any glass got in the pool before we can open for rec swim tomorrow. But it's okay, hon, we'll handle it."

Charlotte's eyes drop. "Oh. Okay."

"Really, don't worry." Lexi tries to smile and appear enthusiastic. "Just be here Monday at seven thirty sharp—first day of morning practice!"

My sixteen-year-old brother climbs out of the lane where the 15–18s practice alongside us. "I didn't see any glass in the water," he says. "But glass is, like, clear, so I might have missed it."

"Jack! Dude!" Lexi scolds. "I told everyone to get out of the water! That means you too."

Jack flashes a smoldering grin. "I'm the lifeguard. It's my duty to keep everyone safe. Rules don't apply to me."

Lexi groans. "Rules have never applied to you, have they?"

"Only when I'm the one making them. Like now." He turns his attention to the swimmers lingering on the deck. "Okay, kids! Wait out on the sidewalk by the parking lot. Unsafe zone here!"

While Jack monitors the kids waiting for parents, Ez and I pull our shorts over our suits and join Lexi on the pool deck. She's checking the whole area up and down, sighing and redoing her thick ponytail every few minutes.

"Find anything else?" I ask.

"No, but it's super weird, because it's two pieces of glass from the same bottle, or whatever it was. Look." She holds up the shards. "They fit together. But where's the rest of it? Like, if someone broke a bottle here, then there would be more pieces, right?"

Ez hops to the side of the pool. "Want me to jump in and see if Jack missed any pieces in the water?"

"No, no." Lexi stops her. "Dad's coming to run the sweep, so if there's any in the pool it should get vacuumed up. Really, you guys should just go."

"Hey, I'm in this family too," I say.

Lexi turns to me. "I know. But this is too stressful for you, Mad. I thought doing a fun practice race would be good for you. You know, get you out of your comfort zone, or whatever. But you should just go home."

"I can handle it." My sister's protectiveness irritates me. I know she wants to keep me from getting too anxious, but other people making decisions about what's good for me makes me even more anxious.

"Yeah, Maddie." Jack towels off his wet hair. "We got this."

"Whatever," I say, but Ez and I make no movements to leave. Instead, we follow Lexi's lead, searching the pool and checking around the bleachers, under chairs and chaise lounges, and all over the large patch of lawn where kids lay their towels and stake tents and pop-ups on meet days.

Just as I feel my breathing slow, my dad rushes onto the pool deck with a burst of frantic energy, face flushed, car keys jingling in his hand.

"Lex, kids, everyone okay?" he says, eyes darting around the pool deck.

Lexi still gingerly holds the glass shards. "Yeah, nobody got hurt."

Dad pockets his car keys and runs a hand through his thinning hair. "Good. But we can't open tomorrow if there's glass anywhere, because there might be glass in the pool, and we can't handle an injury lawsuit right now. So, let's check and double-check, and I'll run the sweep all night. It's not the way I was hoping to start the summer season, but it'll be okay."

Lexi throws the glass in a garbage can, and Ez and I stay a little longer to help check everything. As Ez and I get ready to leave, Lexi and Jack and Dad are still jittery and looking under things they've looked under a hundred times already. Well, Lexi and Dad are jittery. Jack is humming "Shake It Off" while he dances on the bleachers.

Before Ez and I exit the pool area, I get another look at the glass pieces sitting at the top of the garbage can. I pick them up and turn them over in my hands. And I spot what I didn't spot before: the glass is curved and embedded with glitter. It's not glass from a bottle.

It's glass from a heart-shaped snow globe.

Chapter 2

"For the record, I totally could have taken Owen and Aidan. Sophie too," Ez says as we walk down the street toward our houses.

"Obviously! They're probably relieved that race didn't happen. You've been beating them since we were in the 7–8s." I bump her shoulder.

"Yeah. Pretty much. I was beating them back when I still had hair! It's Charlotte that I'm never sure about. She almost had me on those 50s." Ez shakes her head. "But are you okay? You didn't seem super freaked out about the glass, but it was weird, right?"

"Right. I'm okay," I tell Ez, and it's not a lie. "But it wasn't just a glass bottle."

"What do you mean?"

I take a deep breath. "It was the snow globe, Ez. The glass—it was glass from the snow globe that Lucas gave me."

Ez halts in the middle of the sidewalk. "Oh my god, Mad. Really? How do you know?"

"The snow globe had glitter in the glass. And it was curved in a heart shape, like the glass was. I didn't realize it at first because the sun was so bright it just made everything shiny. But then later, when the glass was in the garbage in the shade, I saw it was glittery, and I recognized it." I shudder.

Ez's eyes are giant. "So, do you think Lucas did it? Is he trying to get back at you for rejecting him? Like, get you to step on glass and hurt yourself or something?"

My stomach twists at the idea that Lucas might want to hurt me. "I don't know. I mean, he doesn't really live around here. And he swims for River Oaks now, remember? Since he got kicked off Maple Grove? So, he probably has practice at the same time we do. I don't think he could get it here."

"That is super creepy." Ez shakes her legs like they're covered in bugs.

I hug my arms around my body, chilled despite the hot afternoon sun. "I mean, the glass was shattered all over the sidewalk by the school, which is like a couple blocks from here, so I don't know how it would get from there to here."

Ez meets my eyes. "Okay, so when I first asked if you were okay, I was actually thinking more like is your anxiety okay, but that is way freakier."

Because I tell Ez everything, she knows all about my anxiety, and that I'm on medication that helps me a ton.

Back in third grade, my parents took me to a therapist, but no matter what we did, I couldn't fall asleep at night, and I couldn't get my work done during the day. I was nervous, like, all the time. I missed a lot of school because the anxiety drained my energy. Now the medication helps me get to school and do my work and eat and sleep.

I still get anxious sometimes though. I just have tools that help me handle it now. And thanks to those tools, I don't see the therapist much anymore unless I need to. My regular doctor manages my medication.

"Oh, yeah. That," I say. "Yep, definitely with the anxiety. I mean, even before I realized the glass was from the snow globe, I started to worry about what if we didn't find all the glass? What if someone gets cut? Then they'll sue us, and we'll have no money, and we'll have to close the pool and no swim team and no business and ..."

"Yeah, your anxiety can be intense," Ez says softly. She reaches into her bag and pulls out a baseball hat to keep the sun off her head.

"It can be. But I know how to handle it. You know, the deep breaths, all my art stuff, and the meds help, obviously. I just wish my parents and Lex and Jack would let me handle it instead of tiptoeing around me all the time."

Ez snorts. "They did kind of want you out of there today, huh?" She mimics my family. "*We got it, go home. Don't worry, Maddie.*"

"Thank you! Ugh, yes!" I groan.

"So you're really not going to tell them about Lucas?"

"No way. They would freak out and tell me I can't handle it and probably, like, email his parents or the school principal or something."

Ez laughs. "Yeah, they probably would."

I don't really want to talk about anxiety anymore. Or heart-shaped snow globes. Or my parents and the way they worry too much about me.

"What was up with Charlotte today? She hasn't wanted to race you in a while," I say.

"Huh?" Ez says. "Charlotte? Yeah, I guess she hasn't been as into racing as when we were younger. I think the new age group makes her nervous."

"That's what I was thinking too. Especially the boys in the new age group."

"So true!" Ez snorts. "But she's got to want to race. I mean, we have to be ready for the scholarship people. And I will take every opportunity I can to swim fastest and get that scholarship for the Tomlin training team. If I don't get it, I can't do the team, and there goes my swimming life."

Even though we still have another year before high school, Ez has always dreamed about going to the Tomlin Academy for Athletes, the most elite athletic private high school in town. Tomlin has a competitive program where eighth graders can train with the high school team while competing at a Junior National level. But the Tomlin training team is nearly as expensive as the tuition for the high school, and even though Ez's mom works really hard managing a popular restaurant, it's not enough. Ez can't join the Tomlin team without a scholarship.

"You've been dying to go there since third grade." I'll

be going to the public high school, but I haven't thought that much about it yet.

"Yep. First Tomlin, then the Olympics!" Ez hoots as we stop in front of her house.

"You can do it. This is your summer." I raise my hands in triumph as I walk backward toward my house.

"Best. Summer. Ever. Mad, I can feel it!" Ez shouts. "I mean, as long as we don't find any more broken snow globes."

"Whatever. We can handle those." I desperately want Ez to have her best-ever summer. The only problem is that there's only one scholarship at Tomlin for the training team.

And there's one other person who wants it: Charlotte.

∎

"Lex! Did you drink all the milk?" Jack hollers on Saturday morning like he's the only person in the universe. I'm still in bed, but my first day of summer won't include sleeping in.

"No, dude, there's another carton behind the juice," I hear Lexi respond. "Maybe try actually looking for something you can't find instead of just opening the fridge and expecting it to jump into your hands?" I can almost hear Lexi rolling her eyes.

I reach for my sketchbook to see if I can get down the scene I had been dreaming about. It had something to do with polar bears vying for spots at an elite teddy bear training school.

The front door slams. If I weren't already awake, Dad's booming voice in the hallway would have snapped me up. "The sweep is broken. It stopped running at some point during the night. We have to hold off opening today until I can get a repair guy out here and run it at least another hour."

"How much is that going to cost?" I hear Mom ask. I'm not getting any drawing done now that money conversations are happening. That polar bear dream is best forgotten anyway.

Dad mumbles a few things, and then I hear him talking on the phone. I put my sketchbook away in the drawer that thankfully no longer contains a snow globe and shuffle into the kitchen for breakfast.

As I'm pouring milk on my cereal, Dad puts his phone down. "Maddie. Everyone. I need you to do that social media thing. I put a closed-for-repairs sign on the pool gate, but we're gonna be able to open by one. Get on the socials and tell your friends."

"Uh, can I have breakfast first?" I ask through a mouthful of Chocolate Cheerios.

"Yeah, yeah, but get on it." Dad grabs a bagel on his way back out the front door. "I'm headed back to the pool to meet Rick the repairman. Lex and Jack, you're both on at noon to help set up. Maddie, social media—don't forget. One o'clock! One's the word! Snack bar will be open! See everyone at the East Valley pool at one. Post that."

"I think I'll reword that a little, but sure, Dad, I'm

on the socials." I smile into my cereal. Lexi and Jack grumble agreement as they finish their breakfasts and get ready to work.

I open up Instagram Stories and film my cereal bowl as I pour in the milk. On the bowl like a label, I write: *sleep late, eat breakfast, swim. EV pool open at one. be there.*

I hesitate for a second before posting. I know Lucas still looks at my Instagram. I blocked him, but he has ways of seeing it—through friends' accounts or something. Do I really want someone who's mad enough to smash glass knowing where I am today?

But it's the first day of summer and my family owns a pool. It wouldn't take a genius or an Instagram story to know where I'll be today. I go ahead and post.

Then I open our swim team's group chat with Ez, Charlotte, and a couple other 13–14s and text:

> Me: hey pool opening late today
> dad says 1:00 spread the word

Within five seconds, Ez writes back.

> Ez: is it ok? that's late for first day of
> summer

> Me: yeah had to vacuum extra all
> good by one

> Charlotte: on it

> Me: yr the best

And she is. Charlotte's social media presence is legendary. She's had two videos go viral, so she has like fifteen thousand followers on TikTok and almost as many on Instagram. She does all her TikToks in her racing suit and cap and goggles. It's her thing. She's actually pretty funny and even pretty effective.

As I'm finishing up my cereal, my notifications bing, and I check TikTok. Charlotte's there in her dark-blue racing suit with her cap half on, long blond hair dangling out the bottom. She does a short dance to "Watermelon Sugar" and then says, "East Valley pool opens at one o'clock today. Be there in the afternoon for hot pretzels and cold Popsicles with me!" She holds up a little sign with the name of the club and the address. It's very sweet.

Charlotte also makes a post and a story on Instagram, holding the same sign. It's been up less than three minutes and she has over one hundred views and counting.

Charlotte's posts must have worked, because when I get to the pool at one thirty, it's busy. Jack is on the lifeguard stand, and Lexi and Dad are at the Snack Shack, selling hot dogs, nachos, sodas, soft pretzels, ice cream bars, and lots and lots of candy.

As the afternoon goes on, nearly the entire swim team comes in and out. I text Ez, and she comes over around two, sporting a floppy straw hat to keep her head from burning. Charlotte and her friend Tina, who's not on the team, come over around three wearing bikinis and cute cover-ups, ready to spread the word on the internet that the East Valley pool is the place to be.

While Charlotte and Tina make a TikTok using a water polo ball and three kickboards as props, Ez leans over. "Find any more glass? Or any more snow globe?"

I whisper, "I keep thinking I see more glass in the bushes, but it just turns out to be a plastic wrapper or something. That snow globe haunts my nightmares."

"It was such a weird present." Ez shudders. "But it looks like the pool is doing okay."

"Mostly. I mean, we're having a good day, I think. But I better check and see if Lexi needs Snack Shack help."

"Good, because I'm about to photobomb Charlotte's TikTok. No video is complete without an appearance by this shiny head." Ez pulls her hat off and smears on the sunscreen.

I give Ez a fist bump. "Own it. See you back here in a few."

By the end of the day, I've relieved Lexi at the snack bar three times and helped Jack and Dad clean up at closing. I'm a bit sunburned, but happy. It seems like we had a good day.

But after dinner, I hear Dad and Mom going over the receipts.

"Snack bar did okay, but we missed so many families with the one o'clock start," Mom complains. She does most of the accounting and ordering, as well as teaching a yoga class a few times a week.

Dad looks at the receipts. "It's not our best opening day."

"It's not even in the top ten," Mom says. "Usually, the first Saturday after school's out is a big moneymaker for us. But we lost half a day, and families probably went to other pools or just went home when they saw the closed sign. Plus, Rick's sweep repair fee was nearly half of our snack bar sales for the afternoon."

"I get it," Dad says. "Well, we may have to put off updating the chlorination system and replacing the tile in the locker rooms until next year."

"We may not be able to," Mom says. "One more chip in that ancient tile and we won't pass inspection this year. We've got to have better weekends than this one. It's not like we have an extra ten thousand dollars lying around to do these repairs."

Dad sighs. "We will. It's only the beginning of summer. We won't have any more closed days."

Chapter 3

It's a six-minute walk to the pool from my house. At 7:21 on Monday morning, I cruise through the club gates and immediately stop in my tracks. Lexi and Jack aren't in the water setting up the lane lines like they should be. They're mopping the pool deck.

"What happened?" I ask. A few other swimmers trickle through the gate behind me.

Jack says, a little too loudly, "Just a spill, no worries. Go ahead and get ready for practice. Nothing to see here, folks. Keep it moving."

I glance at a glob of yellow at my feet. "That's not a spill. That's an egg." I crunch the corner of a shell under my flip-flop. "We got egged?" My stomach drops.

"Shh!" Jack puts his arm around my neck in more of a brotherly headlock than a brotherly hug. "We don't want everyone to know."

"Why?" I croak.

Lexi sighs. "Because we don't need the drama, and we don't need people thinking we're gonna close or cancel practice again."

"Um, okay, but why would we cancel practice just for eggs?" I push Jack's arm off me so I can speak.

"We wouldn't unless they got in the pool. Which, as far as we can tell, they didn't." Lexi sounds exasperated. "But move your feet, and throw that shell away, please?"

"Did I just step in egg? Ew!" Charlotte hollers from behind me.

"So much for keeping it quiet," I mumble, and pick up the shell.

Charlotte skips over to Lexi. "Is practice canceled?"

Jack points at the fence line. "Nope. The fence is higher next to the pool for exactly this reason. So people won't throw stuff in the pool from outside the gate."

Charlotte spins around to look at the fence on her way to the locker room. "Huh, that's smart."

Ez pushes through the gate. "Aw, no, is practice canceled?"

"It's okay," I tell her. "C'mon, let's go."

While Ez and I walk to the locker room, I pull her close and whisper, "It's Lucas. He egged us."

"What?" She grabs my arm. "How do you know?"

"I just know. Or actually, I don't know. But I think. I mean, he was mad enough to smash glass all over the sidewalk and then maybe bring that glass to the pool. He's mad at me, and he wants me to know it."

"I could totally see him doing this, but maybe it wasn't him, Mad. I mean, last day of school and everything this weekend—people love a little light egging." Ez shrugs.

Sophie and a few other swimmers walk past us, so

I lean close to Ez and whisper, "This is a big deal." An itchy shiver runs over my arms. "He's out of control."

Ez meets my eyes. "Nobody got hurt though. If it was him, let's hope he just wanted to blow off some steam and now he's done. And maybe it wasn't even him."

"I guess." I follow her through the doors of the girls' locker room. "I mean, first week of summer does make everyone act like wild animals. I guess it could have been, like, graduation parties gone bad or something."

"Right," Ez says. "Could be anyone."

I'm not sure if that makes me feel better or worse. The idea that Lucas wants to trash my family's club makes me feel guilty, like if I'd just kept the annoying snow globe, he'd leave us alone. But I don't like the idea that some other random person is throwing eggs at our club either.

"I guess you're right." I sigh. "And since Jack and Lexi and probably my parents want to keep it quiet, we'll never even talk about it again."

Ez and I stash our stuff in cubbies. The locker room doesn't have any actual lockers, just benches, cubbies, three shower stalls, and four bathroom stalls. And a floor full of faded green tile that's cracked in a bunch of places and even chipped in a few. My mom is right— it does look like it needs replacing before the yearly inspection.

"Well, whatever. It's over now, so we better get in," Ez says. I grab my towel and cap and goggles and follow her onto the pool deck.

It's 7:28 when I stick my feet in the water and fold my hair into my cap. When Lexi hollers, "Everyone in! Two hundred warm-up, let's go!" I know she has no intention of talking about the eggs again. It'll be like it never happened.

But when I leave after practice, I spy something white under one of the bushes by the gate. At first, I think it's just more eggshell, but when I look closer, I can see that it's a tiny polar bear, torn from an embrace.

It's one of the hugging bears from the snow globe. My heart pounds. I check to see if there's any glass around the bear, and I don't see any. But that doesn't make sense. Did Lucas throw the bear over the fence when he threw the eggs? Or has the bear been here ever since the day we found the glass? I check again for any shards.

I shudder. Why does that miserable snow globe keep coming back to haunt me? I gave it back so I wouldn't have to deal with it anymore. Now it won't leave me alone.

I scoop up the bear and zip it into the little inside pocket of my bag where I keep things I don't want everyone to see. I'll figure out what to do with it later.

For at least two days following the egging incident, the East Valley Athletic Club feels like summer is supposed to feel—no one mentions money, or glass, or eggs, or polar bears.

I don't tell my family that the glass was from the snow globe, or that I found the bear after the egging. I don't want to go into the whole story about Lucas and have them worry that I can't handle some obnoxious boy who has a crush on me. They worry about me enough. And I don't want to think about Lucas anymore. I gave him back his present. I should have a fun summer and not worry about him, like Ez said.

Wednesday evening is warm and dry, and a handful of us swimmers gather at the pool. It doesn't get dark until almost nine. So, during the week, the pool stays open until eight thirty. Dad's running the barbecue, filling the chlorinated air with the scent of grilled meat. Half the swim team is here, buying burgers and hanging out. This is the fun part about my family owning a pool in the summertime. It's like every night is a party.

The polar bear is still zipped into my practice bag, which is tucked away at home. Tonight, I brought my beach bag. I've managed to keep that bear out of sight and mostly out of mind, and I'd like it to stay that way.

Jack watches the scene from the lifeguard stand, repeatedly blowing his whistle and yelling, "Walk, please!" Several high school girls lounge on the chaises near the stand, watching Jack and acting like they're not.

Ez and Charlotte are in the pool with the other 13–14s playing boys-against-girls water volleyball. Aidan and Owen are on the other side with a handful of boys. I'm sitting on a blanket with a book.

"Char! Your ball!" Ez hollers from the pool.

"Oops," Charlotte says, and does a little pirouette. I think she's more interested in flirting with the boys they're playing against than actually winning the game. Ez is getting super irritated because, Ez being Ez, she wants to win.

"So, are we actually trying to win this game?" Ez grumbles at Charlotte and the other girls.

Charlotte frowns at her and flips her wet ponytail. "I don't want to work too hard—I have to save my energy for practice tomorrow so I can beat you in all of Saturday's races and then post my amazingness on the internet."

"Never gonna happen, Char!" Ez elbows Charlotte, who yelps dramatically.

Owen hollers from the other side, "Are you gonna serve that ball?"

Ez spins the ball in her hands. "Eh, I think we're done. Early practice, you know how it goes. Next point wins?"

I pick at a chunk of yellow in the grass. I guess Jack and Lexi didn't get all of the egg out. Between the volleyball game and the way my mind wanders to Lucas and the egging, I'm not getting much reading done.

As Ez serves the ball, a tall, dark-haired kid walks through the gate and into the pool area. He's wearing jeans and doesn't look like he has a bag with a suit in it. He also looks a little cute, if a little lost. No one wears jeans to a swimming pool. I'm not even sure he knows what happens at a swimming pool. I've never seen him before, but Aidan and Owen definitely have.

"Nicoooo! You came! Where's your suit?" they holler from the water.

Nico shrugs and nervously shifts his feet. "Next time." He looks around for a place to sit near the volleyball game. Most of the lounge chairs are covered in towels and damp stuff. The problem with hanging out at a pool is that everything is wet.

Except the clean, dry, roomy blanket I happen to be comfortably lounging on. Also, I'd pulled a soft orange sundress over my suit when I got out, and my hair is up in a messy bun, so I look mostly dry.

Nico walks over to my blanket. "Um, it looks like all the chair-things are taken. Can I sit here?"

"Sure." My heart takes a tiny leap. Nico smiles, and it's more than just a little cute.

"Hi," he says, "I'm Nico."

"So I heard." I point to myself. "Maddie."

Nico folds his long legs to sit cross-legged at the edge of my blanket. A few butterflies take off in my stomach, and I wonder if I'm about to have a crush.

"Hi, Maddie," he says. "How come you're not swimming?"

I set my book down. "That volleyball game you're watching got out of hand. I get enough competition at meets on Saturdays, and practices. I don't really need more random competition on a Wednesday night." Apparently, the butterflies are making me extra chatty.

"Makes sense." He picks up my book. "So, what are you reading?"

"Hey! Don't lose my place!" I lunge for my book and replace the bookmark that was tucked in the back.

"*Always and Forever, Lara Jean*?" Nico lifts an eyebrow. "Sounds romantic."

"It is! You know, from the To All the Boys series?"

"Never heard of it."

I drop my mouth in fake astonishment. "So, Nico, who I've never seen before and who comes to a swimming pool with no swimsuit and has never heard of To All the Boys. Have you been living under a rock your whole life?"

"No. Minnesota. I just moved here last week." He picks at the grass.

"Ah. Do they even have pools in Minnesota?" I grin. I would wink, but that's so cheesy.

"Yeah, but they're all indoors." He stares at me with deep chocolate-brown eyes, and I think I actually melt a little.

"So, um, okay, Nico from Minnesota," I stammer. "How come Owen and Aidan act like you're their BFF if you just moved last week?"

Nico shrugs. "Aidan's my cousin. Our moms are sisters, and we were born like a month apart. Now we get to go do eighth grade together."

"That's fun," I say. "But it kind of sucks to move right before the last year of middle school."

"It's okay. I think I'm going to like California." He

gives me a huge grin, and my stomach completely melts to somewhere down around my knees.

And then we're interrupted by Owen hollering, "Incoming!" while a soaking-wet Aidan tackles Nico. Owen and the rest of the boys dogpile on top of them. It's like they're toddlers. I hop off the blanket and hold my book away from the potential water damage. I can't help but giggle though. I hang out at the pool so much; I can't get mad when stuff gets wet.

"It never ends with you guys!" I pull a dry towel out of my bag.

The boys are in a soggy heap on my blanket, laughing hysterically.

"Sorry, Maddie!" Aidan yells. "I was just so excited to see my favorite cousin here! At the East Valley pool!" He hops up and gives me a wet hug, then sits back down and puts his arm around a slightly stunned Nico. "You did meet Nico, right? He's moving here."

"Uh-huh." I laugh. "We met." Looks like I'll be putting that blanket in the dryer tonight.

Nico coughs from under Aidan's arm. "So, I guess this is why you wear a swimsuit to the pool even if you don't plan on swimming?"

"Dude!" Owen cackles. "Welcome to California! Swimsuits are for everywhere!" He stands up and offers Nico a hand.

Nico rises, dark patches all over his clothes where the boys soaked him. He's not mad, and it's not cold, but I hand him a towel anyway.

"Thanks." He laughs and wipes his forehead.

The girls climb out of the pool, and Ez grabs her towel and plops on the chaise she'd saved next to my blanket.

I turn to her. "So, game over?"

Ez sighs. "Yeah, it's almost closing time anyway."

Charlotte slides up next to me and whispers, "Who's the cute new boy?" She towels off her bright two-piece suit and perches on the end of Ez's chaise.

"What cute new boy?" Of course, I know exactly who she's talking about. "Oh, you mean Nico? He's Aidan's cousin."

"Interesting." Charlotte says as she looks Nico up and down before shaking out her hair. I can't tell if she said that because she's interested in him, or if she's just checking to see how he'd look in a TikTok. I hope she's not interested in him.

From the lifeguard stand, Jack blows his whistle. "Ten minutes to close!"

"Aw, man," Owen groans. "I was just about to push Minnesota in the pool."

Nico shoves Owen's shoulder. "Like I'm not wet enough!"

I wring out my sopping blanket while everyone else wraps towels around their waists and gathers their things. Even if my friends are leaving, I'll be staying a while longer to help Dad and Jack clean up.

As the boys get ready to go, Nico turns to me. "Bye, Maddie. Thanks for sharing your blanket."

I smile. "Anytime."

"Really? Anytime?" He grins wide and walks backward toward the pool gate.

Aidan throws an arm around his cousin. "Dude. You've been here like five minutes and you're already flirting with the cutest girls!"

The butterflies multiply in my stomach, and I look down to hide my blush. But I can't hide my smile.

I think Nico's blushing too, because he stammers, "Sorry about, uh, my cousin. See you around?"

I can't stop smiling. "It's okay, I'm used to Aidan being all up in everyone's business. And, yeah, if you hang out with these two, you'll see me around. We're always here."

Chapter 4

At least, I thought we would always be there. But when I arrive at the pool the next morning for practice, I know something's wrong.

A couple of swimmers are gathered at the gate. "We're not supposed to go in yet," someone says.

But I don't listen. I push my way through the gate and onto the pool deck. My throat catches. All I can see is some kind of red goo smeared over the concrete. My first thought goes to the glass. Did we not find all of it? Did someone cut themselves? Did the rest of the snow globe attack our pool? All I see is red, red, red.

I look again. It's not blood. It's too much and too goopy. There's something yellow too. I wonder if it's more eggs, but it's not the right shade. Lexi stands over the red-and-yellow mess with her hands on her hips. She looks tired and still has a little eyeliner on from her date last night with her girlfriend, Kari.

"What happened? What's going on?" I take a step toward her.

"No, Maddie, stay there!" Lexi says, looking up. But she moves too quickly. Her foot slips in the red goo and she goes down hard on her hip.

My stomach drops.

"Be careful," Lexi gasps. "Don't come closer. Just call Dad and go outside and wait. This is going to freak you out."

Now I'm mad. This is like when my family fast-forwards through the scary parts of a movie because they want to protect me.

They can't fast-forward this. I inch closer to the goo. A whiff of something tomatoey and cheesy hits my nose. "Oh my god, is that ketchup all over the pool deck? And nacho cheese?"

"Yep, and mustard. And it's really slippery."

My stomach turns, but I'm so relieved it's not blood. "Oh my god. Are you okay?"

Lexi shifts her weight to her other hip and gently rubs her injury. "I'll live, it's just a bruise. I'm just glad I got here first, and it wasn't one of you. Really, you should wait outside."

"Come on, Lex. I'm not going to explode. Let me get you ice."

She sighs. "Fine. Be really, really careful."

I avoid the mess by walking around the pool to the locker room, where I can go into the clubhouse kitchen. But when I'm on the side of the pool, I see what I couldn't see before: words. The ketchup is all over the place, the nacho cheese is sort of in splotches, but in the middle of the huge smear of ketchup are the words EELS SUCK written in mustard.

My heart races. This has to be Lucas again, getting

back at me. But it's such a mess. It looks like it took a bunch of people to pull off a prank like this. I don't know if he could make a mess this big on his own.

"Lexi! Did you see what this says?" I holler.

She's still sitting in ketchup on the other side of the pool. I don't know if her hip is too painful to stand on, or if she just can't figure out what to do. "Yeah. I saw it. And I saw what's in the pool too." She points to a few brown chunks in the deep end next to a smear of ketchup.

"Oh no. Is that . . . code brown? Gross! *Why?*" I cough. Could this morning get any worse?

I take a deep breath and try to even out my rapid breathing. I wasn't lying when I told Lexi I could handle it, but this is worse than I thought. And, like the egging, this was no accident. Someone came into our pool and made a slippery, dangerous mess that actually injured my sister. Someone who could be getting back at me.

Meanwhile, poop and ketchup in the pool mean another day of vacuuming and no practice.

Plus, they wasted two jumbo-sized canisters of ketchup, a tub of nacho cheese, and a squirt bottle of mustard. That's a lot of condiments we need for the Snack Shack. The broken containers sit in the garbage can next to the locker room, which is weird. Who would make such a mess and then actually throw away the garbage?

I take out my phone and text Dad. I don't say much, just that the pool has been vandalized and to get here soon.

When I return from getting ice, Jack is analyzing Lexi's injury. I hand Lexi the ice and tell the rest of my teammates to go home. Most of them are happy to get back to their beds, but not before stepping through the gate long enough to get a glimpse of the pool deck.

I hear a few rounds of "That's ketchup, not blood, right?" and "Ew, poo in the pool!" before my brother takes over crowd control.

"Dudes. Everyone. Nothing to see here." Jack waves his arms and ushers everyone out, then turns to me. "I'm gonna stay at the gate and keep kids from coming in. You can go home."

I prickle at the idea of being sent home mid-crisis. Again. "I'll stay with Lexi until Dad gets here."

Jack shrugs. "Okay. But you don't have to." He focuses on the other swimmers, who linger at the gate. "Guys! No practice today. Yeah, no, all good. No worries."

Eventually, the rest of the swimmers exit the area, trading theories about what could have possibly happened on the pool deck.

By the time Dad arrives, all but one of the swimmers have left.

I'm not sure how Ez got past Jack the gatekeeper, but she appears at my side while I'm scanning the water for more unexpected surprises.

"So, no practice?" Ez asks, though she clearly knows the answer.

"Yeah." I point at the water. "Code brown." Then I point to the pool deck. "And code slimy ketchup."

"Ew." Ez wrinkles her nose. "I was going to complain about no practice, but this is way worse."

I lead Ez around to the other side of the pool. "You haven't seen the actual worst of it yet. You can only see it from this side." The ketchup-cheese-mustard mess is smeared from Lexi's fall and Dad's inspection, but the words are still mostly readable.

"Does that say 'Ez Sucks'?" Ez yells. "Oh. No, now I see it says 'Eels Suck.' Still. What the heck? We do not suck. Who would do this?" She lowers her voice. "Was it Lucas?"

My throat tightens, and I feel like I'm going to cry. "I don't know. It could be. It could also be someone on another team. Someone who wants to hurt us so we'll lose. I mean, Lexi's fall was pretty bad, and everyone knows nacho cheese is, like, the most slippery substance ever." I point to Lexi sitting on her bag of ice on a chaise lounge. "Whoever did this wanted to really throw us off our game."

Dad joins us opposite the mess. "Nah, I'm sure it's just a prank. The only damage is on the clubhouse door. Lock's broken."

I gasp. "Someone broke in? Really? That's a lot of work just to tell us we suck. Are you going to call the cops?"

"Already did." Dad frowns. "They're sending someone to take a report. But since nothing valuable appears to be missing or permanently damaged, and no serious injuries . . ."

"Lucky. There could have been," I mumble.

"But there weren't. So, we'll just file a report," Dad asserts.

"Aren't they going to investigate?" Ez asks.

"Investigate? I don't think swim team pranks are high on the police priority list, especially when it doesn't look like more than a bunch of spilled condiments." Dad sighs.

"It's not the first time though, right? The pool got egged, probably by the same person who did this!" I'm almost yelling. Ez looks the other way.

I'm about to tell Dad that I think it was Lucas, but then he puts his hands on his hips and says, "You're not supposed to worry about that."

Just as I thought. My parents don't think I can handle anything. They don't think I can handle Lucas or whatever it is he's doing to our pool. So, I don't say anything. I just bite my lip and try not to cry.

Dad shakes his head. "Maddie, you need to let this go. You, too, Esmeralda. And if you want to get in a workout, come this afternoon. I'll have this all cleaned up by then. Focus on your races, not this."

It's useless to argue with my family when they're trying to protect me. But I am not about to let this go. I grit my teeth and get my things, following Ez toward the gate.

"You good?" I ask Lexi as I pass her.

Lexi opens one eye. "Yeah, Mad, it's fine. Don't worry."

Don't worry, Maddie. It's always *Don't worry, Maddie*. At least Ez doesn't mind worrying me.

"Are you okay?" I ask Ez when I reach her. She's pretty jumpy. I wonder if the "Eels Suck" sentiment got to her.

"Yeah, are you?"

"I guess?" I kick the gate closed behind us. "I mean, is it okay that I might have a stalker who likes to trash my family's pool? No. But am I going to have a full-on meltdown? Also no. I just want to know for sure who did it."

"Don't do anything without me." Ez grabs my arm. "I have to try to get some training in, but I'll come over tomorrow and help you get ready for the meet, and investigate. We'll see if anyone's posted anything online or if any clues turn up. Whoever did this will let something slip eventually."

"Ooh, like real Nancy Drews! I'll see if I can find a magnifying glass." I don't feel like I might cry anymore.

"Yes! And a flashlight and maybe some code-breaking devices. Not that we have any codes to break, but Nancy would be prepared for the unexpected. You ready?" Ez's eyes sparkle. "'Cause we are on the case of the East Valley Vandal!"

I have to laugh, which is a relief after being so close to tears. "Thanks for that. So, what's with the urge to get training in? We've been having good practices."

"Yeah. But so has Charlotte." Ez exhales loudly. "I mean, my practice is nothing compared to extreme ketchup-code-brown vandalism, but if I don't have a great meet this weekend, those scholarship people are going to pay more attention to her."

"Does Charlotte even need the scholarship?" I wonder. "Can't her parents afford Tomlin without it?"

Ez shrugs. "I don't even know if it's about money. I think Charlotte's parents just like it when she wins things."

"I think Charlotte also likes it when she wins things, especially if she can tell the world about it. But yeah, her parents are a little, uh, involved, huh?" We turn the corner onto our street.

"They always have been," Ez says. "It's weird. I mean, my mom is super supportive, but I always felt like it was because she knew I wanted it so bad, not because she wanted it for me."

"And because your natural talent is so obvious." I bump Ez's hip as we walk.

"Hey!" Ez stops. "Maybe that's it! Maybe the prank today, and the egging, wasn't Lucas at all. Maybe it was someone who doesn't want me or Charlotte to get that scholarship."

"I thought no one else was up for the scholarship?" I point out. "Plus, it did say 'Eels Suck,' so it seems like an attack on the whole team."

"Yeah, you're right," Ez says. "Okay. So, it has to be another team. Or Lucas. Or both, since Lucas is on another team. We should talk to your dad. Tell him our theories."

I sigh. "My dad doesn't want me to worry about it. He just wants me to be happy and not think about this kind of thing."

Ez's eyes bore into mine. "Fine. That means we have to look into it. Whether it's Lucas or another team, or whatever. *We* have to figure out who's trying to sabotage the Eels."

Chapter 5

On Friday night, Ez comes over to help me pack my things for the meet tomorrow. Or, more specifically, to keep me company while I pack. She paces back and forth in my room, while I sit on my bed and tuck the necessary items into my bag.

"So, I have to show you something and you're not going to like it," she says. "It doesn't mean Lucas did it, but maybe it might."

"What? You've been holding out evidence?" I throw an extra pair of goggles into the duffel bag.

"I'm not really holding out. I didn't see it until today." Ez grimaces.

"Oh my god, show me."

"Okay, so you didn't see this because you blocked Lucas, but . . ." Ez holds up her phone.

It's Lucas's latest Instagram post: a picture of him making a gross face under his floppy bleached hair. The caption reads: *poo + kechup in the pool at East Valley this morning ew* followed by several poo emojis.

"What? How did he know?" My face gets hot. "I mean, my dad said the deck was clean by like ten a.m.

The code brown takes longer with the vacuuming and stuff, but still."

"Well, everyone in our age group got a glimpse of the mess, so I guess it got around," Ez says.

"I can't believe he posted that! Does that mean he did it?" I throw my team cap into my bag a little too vigorously.

"I dunno." Ez runs her hand over her head. "I mean, if he did it, I don't think he would post about it."

"Even if he didn't do it, what a jerk to post that," I grumble.

"Totally."

"So . . ." I pick up my bag. The bag that still has the single polar bear zipped into the inner pocket. "I've been holding out evidence too."

"What? Spill." Ez stops pacing.

"You know the polar bears from the snow globe? Look." I hold out the bear in the palm of my hand. "I found this in the bushes on the day we got egged."

Ez's eyes grow wide. "Oh. My. God. Maddie. It was Lucas then! I mean, did he throw that in the club when he threw in the eggs?"

"I don't know. I don't know how long it had been there before I found it. Maybe it had been there as long as the glass. I didn't tell anyone because I didn't want to have to tell them about the snow globe." I zip the bear back into its hidden pocket. "I should have just kept the globe."

"No, definitely not. You did the right thing giving

it back. The actual right thing would have been him never giving it to you in the first place." Ez paces again. "Anyway, first there's glass from the snow globe on the deck, then there's the bear from the snow globe with the eggs, then Lucas posts about a ketchup vandalism. I don't know, Mad, Lucas seems like he can't let something go."

My stomach lodges in my throat. "Is he . . . is he stalking me?"

Ez leaps to sit at my side. "I don't know. Are you going to tell your parents about the bear?"

"No way," I say. "I don't know what it means, and involving my parents would mean telling them all about Lucas. They already think I'm too anxious to deal with anything. I don't want to prove them right. Let's just handle this ourselves."

"Okay. If you say so." Ez scrunches her nose. "Let's focus on River Oaks since Lucas is on that team and we swim against them tomorrow. It could also be a team we meet later, like Maple Grove. That team is ruthless, and they hate losing."

I snort. "Yeah. They do. And Lucas is connected to that team too."

Lucas was on the Maple Grove team a couple of years ago when Ez, Charlotte, and the 11–12s free-relay team pulled out a win in one of the last events of the day. Lucas and some other Maple Grove kids set off the alarm on the chlorine gas tanks, and we all had to evacuate the pool area immediately.

Chlorine tanks have alarms that go off if they leak, and like glass on the pool deck, it's one of those things coaches freak out about. Apparently, inhaling chlorine gas can make you really sick. But the alarm got turned off quickly, and no one got hurt. No one even smelled anything weird.

We learned Lucas was the one who did it because he bragged about it all through sixth grade. I'm pretty sure he thought he was being cool. But it was really just annoying, and it got him kicked off his swim team.

It was right around then that he started having a crush on me. It was like he thought he could impress me by doing this wild prank. He'd mention it every time he saw me. He'd also message me all the time on Instagram.

I take a deep breath. "Okay, so I still think it was Lucas. He has motive—to get back at me for not liking him. And I think he did the glass and the egging too. But how would he have gotten the snow globe glass into the pool area?" I fold an extra towel and tuck it in my bag. "We would have seen him, right?"

"Maybe he just ran in and out between practices. I mean, if it was after the 11–12s and before our practice, there are so many kids going in and out that no one would have noticed someone who wasn't on our team. He even could have gotten someone to do it for him." Ez stops pacing to stare at one of my paintings on the wall. "I like this one. Looks like water. Anyway, we don't really know when the glass actually got under the block. We only found it because Char and I wanted to race."

"Yeah, I guess." I smile at her quick compliments on my painting and tuck a change of clothes into my bag. "And the eggs and the ketchup—he, or whoever, could have done that the night before. Like, anytime. The neighborhood doesn't have any security really."

"Right, security. What did the cops say to your dad?" Ez asks.

"Not much." I shrug. "Or maybe Dad didn't want to tell me much. He just said they took a report but since nothing major was stolen it was probably—his favorite phrase—just a prank. I don't even think he told them about the eggs."

"Which means they're not going to do anything about it." Ez resumes pacing back and forth on my sea-blue rug.

"Yeah, I guess not." I look again at Lucas's post. It's so gross. "Um, Charlotte didn't post about anything that happened, did she? I mean, I don't think she would go against us like that, but she does love social media attention."

Ez takes her phone back. "Yeah, she does. But no, she hasn't posted anything today. And it looks like Owen and Aidan tried to get Lucas to take his post down." She shows me a couple of comments from @owwu08 and @aidandabet153 telling Lucas his post is rude.

"Aw, that's nice." I smile.

"Yeah, Owen and Aidan are nice guys. Since like, forever." Ez gets a little grin on her face. "So, what's up with Aidan's cousin? Nico? He seemed pretty chatty with you on Wednesday."

I feel a blush creep over my skin. "He's nice."

"And he's cute," Ez comments.

"Yeah, he's cute." My stomach flutters just thinking about how cute he is. "And he's not pushy, you know, like Lucas. He's just nice."

"So, are we going to be seeing him around? What's his deal? He swim?" Ez folds her legs under her and sits on the bed.

I shrug. "I don't know. I know he's not a swimmer, but I think he'll be hanging around with Aidan and Owen at least until school starts. So yeah, we'll see him."

So far, Ez has only had a few mild crushes on guys in our class. She doesn't really flirt or show a lot of interest in guys. Sometimes people think she's gay because of her lack of hair, which is pretty funny since your hair has nothing to do with who you're attracted to.

Sometimes people think she's sick because of her lack of hair too—like she has cancer or something. People make a lot of judgments about Ez without knowing anything about her. I think she doesn't have a lot of crushes because she's really focused on swimming and getting into the Tomlin training program. She doesn't really have time for crushes. And she's definitely not sick.

"So, is cute Nico going to be at the meet tomorrow?" Ez moves to stand in front of the water painting again.

"I don't know. Maybe." I half smile, zipping up my

bag and stashing it near my bedroom door. It's not that I don't want to talk about Nico, I just don't know yet if I like him. And with everything that's been happening with Lucas, I don't want to act like I like him until I'm sure. I turn the conversation back to the meet. "So, what's our plan for tomorrow? Try to get Lucas to confess?"

"Maybe just see if we can get information, find out where he was on Wednesday night." Ez touches the LED lights circling my walls.

I shiver at the thought of seeing Lucas on the opposing team tomorrow. "He's going to think I want to go out with him if I ask him what he does at night. Gross."

"Okay, I'll ask him," Ez suggests. "Or maybe we can just ask around, see if any of his teammates know anything."

"That sounds much better than actually talking to Lucas."

"Also, we should kick their butts in the races. This has me all fired up." Ez hops from foot to foot.

"We should do that anyway." I let myself smile.

"Yeah, which means I should get home and pack my stuff so I'm ready."

When I walk Ez downstairs and say goodbye, Mom and Dad are in the dining room, talking quietly.

I close the door behind Ez softly. I don't want to interrupt my parents, and I also don't want them to know I'm here. They're talking about the pool and they sound stressed.

"We're just not making the numbers, Mark," my mom says.

"We'll make it up, I know we will. Summer's just begun." My dad's voice is weak.

"But the beginning of the summer is the biggest time. We lost money opening day because of the glass, then word got out yesterday about the cleanup situation, and both yesterday afternoon and today had lower numbers than normal. No one wants to swim in a pool that's had poop in it, or work out in a clubhouse that can get broken into so easily. Thank goodness we managed to keep the egg incident under wraps." Mom's voice is firm.

"I know," Dad says. "But we can make it up. I'm not going to sell out to some big weight-machine company over a couple of slow days."

"I'm just saying listen to what this guy at FitWest has to say," Mom says. "They might really be good for us. Jack will be looking at colleges next year. FitWest could buy the whole club and make a better profit than us, and still pay us to run the thing."

FitWest? FitWest is a big statewide gym. Is my mom saying that FitWest wants to buy the East Valley Athletic Club and turn it into a chain gym? I don't know what that means, but it doesn't sound good. My heart pounds.

"Yeah, and they'd rip out the racquetball courts for high-end gym equipment. What would our Senior Squashers have to say about that?" I can hear Dad's heart breaking. "And big gyms don't sponsor swim teams. FitWest would mean the end of the Eels. We're a community club, Kim. The community needs us."

What do they mean "end of the Eels"? This conversation is not good for my anxiety. But it's worse that they didn't even tell me the pool was having so much trouble.

"FitWest could fix the locker room floors. It could manage the updates we need to do to stay in business," Mom insists. "We might be able to make up some money this summer, but can we make up ten thousand dollars to pay for repairs in order to pass our safety inspections? I don't think so."

"But we don't have as many expenses now. You know, personally. Since Lexi's living here instead of on campus, and we're not paying for Maddie's therapist anymore? We can save for repairs," Dad points out.

"I thought we wanted to keep money available for the therapist just in case?" Mom says.

My fists clench, and I burst into the kitchen. "I don't need a therapist anymore! And I especially don't need one if we need the money for the pool."

My mom jumps out of her seat. "Oh, honey, no. We're not—no."

My dad has his face in his hands. "You weren't supposed to hear that."

"Well, I did." My face gets hot. "So, what's the deal?"

Mom sits back down, and I take a seat opposite her. "We've had an offer from FitWest to purchase the club," she says. "It's a lot of money."

"And we're low on money, aren't we?" I feel like I might cry.

"We've had a rough start to the summer," Mom says. "And since we have repairs to do before the inspection this fall, we really needed to have a good year."

"I thought we were doing okay. I mean, not great, but pretty good," I stammer.

"We are," Mom says. "Just not good enough, with the closed days."

"It doesn't help that someone's trying to sabotage the team." I'm not ready to tell my parents who I think that someone might be. I don't have any proof, and they probably wouldn't believe me. Anyway, they would definitely tell me not to worry about it.

"No, this ketchup thing was just a prank. Just kids," Dad says. Mom nods in agreement.

"Yeah, kids who don't want us to practice," I mutter. "We'll find proof of who did it. Then they won't do it again and we can keep our club."

"No, Maddie," Dad says. "It was just some kid. Nothing serious."

"Or maybe it was your precious FitWest that no one wants to talk about!" I'm almost yelling.

Mom and Dad stare at me in silence. And it hits me: What if it *was* FitWest? What if it wasn't Lucas at all? What if FitWest is trying to put us out of business so they can buy our club?

"Maddie?" Mom asks. "Are you okay?"

"I'm fine. Fine enough that I don't need to go back to therapy and risk losing our entire club."

"Oh, Mad . . ." Mom starts.

"Whatever. I'm going to bed."

I storm up the stairs and get ready for bed, even though I know I won't sleep. Too anxious. I didn't even ask about my medication. I really hope it's covered by health insurance, because I definitely don't think now is a good time to go off it.

I flop onto my bed in frustration. If I could just prove it was Lucas who vandalized our pool, maybe Mom and Dad would stop talking about selling it. But I don't want to bring up Lucas to them unless I know for sure he did it. I don't want to have to tell them about the annoying snow globe and Lucas's annoying crush. I don't want them thinking they have to protect me from him because I can't handle my anxiety. I've handled my anxiety fine. I've handled Lucas fine too. For two years!

I pull out my phone and take a deep breath. I'm not sure this is a good idea, but I need answers. I open Instagram, and I unblock Lucas. Maybe it's a mistake, but I have to know.

I send Lucas a message:

> Me: i know yr mad but don't take it out on my family

He writes back right away.

Lucas: uh is this about the post?

im not mad

why would i be mad?

I pause. I'm not sure talking to him was a good idea, but it's too late now.

Me: you know, the globe

Lucas: i don't care about that anymore

and it was just a joke

Me: a joke????? my sister got really hurt on that ketchup you put all over our deck.

it's not just a joke

Lucas: hold up i didn't do that i meant the post was just a joke

Me: that wasn't funny either

Lucas: i wasnt even in town when the kechup got in your pool

Me: what do you mean?

Lucas: was on a swim retreat with my new team this whole week

Me: you get retreats?

Lucas: stop blaming me for everything
Maddie yr so self centered

That makes my blood boil. But I want more info.

Me: so how did u even know it
happened?

Lucas: tyler told me

Me: why tho?

Lucas: he thought it was funny so do i

why do you care?

you sound obsessd with me or
something

The last text is followed by a kissing-face emoji. Gross.

I don't know how to reply to that, so I drop my phone. I push the emoji out of my head and think about what Lucas said. If Lucas was away on some retreat, then he really didn't do it.

But I don't trust him. Maybe his team really does get to go on retreats, and maybe he really was gone when our pool got ketchup'd. I don't know, but that's the first thing I'll be trying to find out at the meet tomorrow.

Chapter 6

The last time we were at the River Oaks pool was that horrible meet with the glass accident. We weren't even sure River Oaks would open again after they had just been sued.

But today, everything seems like normal at the River Oaks pool. The sun is already warm at six forty-five in the morning. It's going to be one of those hot days where I'm dry almost as soon as I get out of the pool. The strong chlorine smell floating off the pool mingles with the scent of bacon-and-egg breakfast sandwiches from the direction of the snack bar.

Right now, the breakfast smell is making me nauseous. I have that pit-in-my-stomach feeling that I always get at meets, even after years of doing this. There are just so many people and so much excitement and nerves coming off everyone. But it's worse today since I know Lucas will be here. The memory of his messages last night makes my stomach turn.

Ez slides up next to me. "Ready to get in and warm up before the pool gets jammed?" We'd picked up Ez at six thirty. Her mom will come later. No one should have to get up at six thirty on a summer Saturday if they don't have to. Even moms.

"Might as well get it over with." I shed my sweats and pull my cap and goggles out of my bag.

Warm-ups go quickly, and when we line up for the first relay of the day—the 400 medley—I look around for someone I know who I can ask about Lucas. He's not the only River Oaks swimmer who goes to our school.

The blocks at the top of the pool are a commotion of activity. Parents holding coffee tumblers gather to time and judge our strokes. Our teammates line the edges of the pool, already yelling to cheer us on.

Charlotte's parents are right up at the blocks with us, making sure she has water and is properly stretched. Usually parents watch from the sides of the pool with the rest of the spectators, but Charlotte's always get as close as possible.

Today, Charlotte's parents are glancing around the pool deck and talking way too loudly about the Tomlin scholarship people. It doesn't seem to be helping Charlotte's readiness for the relay. She scowls at them and hisses something I can't hear. It makes me think about the conversation Ez and I had about whether Charlotte needs the scholarship. From the way she's looking at her parents right now, I'm not even sure she wants to swim.

I'm not on Ez's relay team. Ez and Charlotte swim on Medley Team A: Sophie does backstroke, and her girlfriend, Jess, does breaststroke. They're both a year older than us but still in our age group—the 14s of the 13–14s. Ez does fly, and Charlotte anchors the team in free.

I usually swim against our Team A on Medley Team B. I do the breaststroke, and we almost always come in third—the East Valley Team A and the opposing team's Team A battle for first. I don't mind being on Team B. There's way less pressure to win, and less pressure means fewer nerves.

I find the person I'm looking for on River Oaks' Team A, lining up with her relay team right next to mine: Daniella Lopez, swimming the freestyle. She was in my math class last year. I touch her arm. "Hey, Dani."

"Hey, Maddie! How's your summer going?" She smiles wide.

"Pretty good," I answer. But I don't have a lot of time to chat before the race starts. I have to get to the point. "So, do you guys really get retreats?"

"Yeah," Daniella says. "Pretty sweet deal. We do this big overnight trip the week after school gets out. Ashley's dad sponsors the older age groups, and we go out to this resort with like three huge pools. It's practice but it's also, you know, team bonding."

So. Lucas's story holds up. But I need more info. "So, you know Lucas? Lucas Bryce?"

"From school? Yeah, I know him." She gives me a funny look.

"Did he go on the retreat with you?" I feel like I'm interviewing her.

"Everyone goes," Daniella says. Then she pauses. "But, you know, I think he got there late. Like, we all got there on Wednesday afternoon, but we didn't see him until Thursday morning. But boys and girls sleep in different parts of the resort, so he might have gotten there Wednesday night. I really don't know. Why?"

"Um, you know that vandalism that happened at our pool?" I keep my voice low. "Just trying to figure out who was in town when it happened."

Daniella's eyes widen. "You think it was Lucas? He is kind of slimy. I heard his relay team talking about how he gave some girl who wasn't even his girlfriend a heart-shaped snow globe."

I don't have time to respond to that because the announcer calls for the 13–14 girls' medley relay back-strokers to take their marks. All conversation ceases as the race begins.

It's an exciting one. Daniella and River Oaks' Team A are really good—must be all the extra retreat time. I jump in for breaststroke in third place and can see how both Team As are doing. Jess's breaststroke is the weakest link on Team A, so when Ez enters the water for butterfly, our Team A is a full body-length behind River Oaks'.

I finish my breaststroke leg and pull myself out of the water in time to see Ez powering through her fly. By the time Charlotte dives in for the freestyle leg, East Valley's Team A has caught up to River Oaks'. Charlotte and Daniella are neck and neck the whole last lap, but

Charlotte touches first, and the Eels' Team A pulls out the win by half a second. The crowd goes wild. It's a great start to the meet.

I don't have time to talk about my clue gathering until later, when Ez and I sit in the 13–14 tent between events.

"Hey." I bump Ez's elbow. "Did you hear Daniella talking about their retreat?"

"I heard you ask, but I couldn't really hear her. Tell me." Ez snacks on a bag of chips. Unlike me, Ez eats a lot on meet days—everything from healthy bananas and power bars to candy.

"Okay. So, first of all, Lucas messaged me last night. He told me he didn't vandalize our pool because he wasn't even in town," I whisper.

"Lucas messaged you? What does this have to do with Daniella?" Ez leans closer to hear me.

"Hold on, I'm getting there," I say. "So, I unblocked Lucas to yell at him for posting that rude picture. I thought that post meant he did it, and I didn't want him to get away with it. But that's not the important part. The important part is he says he *didn't* do it because he was at the retreat."

"So, it was someone else?" Ez asks. "Dang, now we have to start over with the suspect list, Nancy Drew. Who is the East Valley Vandal?"

"Nope. It could still be him. Because Daniella told me—wait for it—Lucas got to the retreat late. She didn't see him until Thursday morning."

Ez gasps and puts her hand on her chin like Sherlock Holmes. "The plot thickens!"

I push her over. "You goofball!"

"Okay, seriously though. Let's just find Lucas. Get to the source. Have you seen him yet?" Ez looks around at the pop-ups scattered over the grass. The River Oaks pop-ups are on the other side of the pool.

"I don't think so. He must not have done the medley. We should watch the next few 13–14 boys' races and see if he's here. Maybe he came late to the meet, too, like he came late to the retreat. Maybe lateness is his thing."

Ez lights up. "Hey, I think we'll have to talk about this later, 'cause look who's coming."

I look up in time to see Owen and Aidan charging the 13–14 girls' tent. My heart thumps when I see who's behind them, sporting what looks like a new pair of shorts: Aidan's cute cousin Nico.

"Ladies! Way to rock the medley relay!" Owen hollers as he grabs the chips from Ez and starts snacking.

"Hey! Those are my chips!" Ez pushes Owen and laughs. We are clearly done talking about Lucas for now. Nancy Drew will have to wait.

Aidan spreads out on our blanket like a lanky puppy, taking up space and excited to see everyone. He grabs Ez's ankle and gives it a friendly squeeze. "Awesome swim, E."

Nico hovers near me. "So, can I share your blanket again?"

"If you can find a spot that your cousin isn't hogging,"

I tell him. Nico finds a tiny square of blanket not covered by his cousin or something wet. He looks at me for more than a second, and I'm pretty sure I blush. "So, uh," I stammer. "You learned not to wear jeans to a pool, it looks like?"

"Yeah, my mom took me shopping and I now have like ten pairs of shorts and three swimsuits since it sounds like the only thing anyone ever does here in the summer is hang out at pools."

"Well, yeah, what else would we do when this is so much fun?" I gesture to the mess of swim caps, snacks, and abandoned articles of clothing under the pop-up. "What do you do in Minnesota in the summer?"

"Be happy we're not living like polar bears like we do in the winter." He shudders.

"I can't even imagine." I shiver and think about the tiny polar bear that's still zipped in my bag. I hate the cold. I clear my throat and push the idea of polar bears far from my mind. "No, really. What do you do?"

"Hang out at the mall," he says. "Go to movies. If it's nice, go out on lakes."

"Like in a boat?" I ask.

"Yes, in a boat." Nico laughs. "Do you have boats here or are you all such great swimmers you don't even need flotation devices?" He's close enough that he bumps my shoulder playfully. My face feels warm and I know it's not the sun.

"Well, we are good swimmers." I grin, reaching for the sunscreen. "Do you not swim at all?"

Nico shrugs. "Oh, I swim, just not very fast. I'm more of a runner."

"Really? Like, competitively?"

"Eh, I was thinking about going out for cross-country this year," Nico says. "And maybe track in the spring. Cross-country is a little more fun because you get a change of scenery, and you're not just chasing white lines around red dirt."

"I know that feeling!" I laugh. "Sounds like chasing a black line on the bottom of the pool."

"Yeah, it's like that." Nico smiles and meets my eyes, and I get that stomach-flip feeling again.

I might be blushing, so I turn my face and glance at Ez throwing chips at Aidan's and Owen's mouths. Every time one of the guys catches a chip, he cheers like he just won state championship.

Charlotte sits under a tree by herself, grinning and making faces at her phone. Only coaches and one designated team parent are allowed back by the swimmers' tents, so for now, Charlotte is free of parental pressure and can do whatever she wants, which apparently is post videos on social media.

"Hey, Maddie," Owen hollers between chips. "What's the deal with the ketchup on the pool deck? They find out who did it?"

"Um, I don't really think anyone is looking," I reply. I don't want to tell the boys my suspicions about Lucas. Then I'd have to get into the whole snow globe thing, and that's not a conversation I want to have around a guy I think I have a crush on.

"What?" Aidan reacts in surprise. "No one is investigating the vandalism at our favorite pool?"

I pick at a loose thread on my blanket. "Yeah, they just think it was a prank or whatever, not a big deal."

I'm relieved to be interrupted by the announcer. "13–14 girls' and boys' 50-yard butterfly to the ready bench! 13–14 fly to the ready bench!"

Ez pops up. "Oh! We gotta go!"

Charlotte croons from the corner, "I'm not doing fly today, so anyone who wants to stay here in the shade with me can join my next TikTok." I think she's looking at Nico, but I try to ignore her.

Nico doesn't even hear her. "Can I watch you swim?" he says to all of us, but I feel like he's really asking me.

Owen punches his shoulder. "Yeah, dude, but please put some sunscreen on your Minnesota face."

"Hey, this face is half-Latino and tans like a dream," Nico replies.

"Oh, so it's red because you're sitting next to Maddie, then?" Aidan lifts his eyebrows and gives Nico a friendly push.

I don't know if Nico's face is red or not, but I'm sure mine is. I grab my cap and goggles and loop my arm through Ez's. "Ready bench?"

She rubs more sunscreen on the top of her head. "Let's do this."

As we walk, I glance behind me. Nico is watching us and gives me a little wave. My heart skips, and I really don't care how well my butterfly race goes.

Chapter 7

When I get out of the pool after the race, Mom is right there with my towel. I don't even have time to look around and see if Nico was watching. "Great job, hon," Mom says. "Can I buy you a bagel?"

I'm still a little mad about the conversation I overheard last night, but I checked my time on the boards and my fly race was decent, so I'm feeling pretty good. Not like Ez, who won first place *and* got a personal record, but decent.

And I do want a bagel. My earlier nausea has been absorbed by race adrenaline, and I'm starving.

"Sure," I tell my mom, and follow her to the snack bar.

After we get my bagel and schmear it up, she walks with me partway back to the 13–14 tent. "I just wanted to make sure you're okay," she says. "You know, after what you heard last night, about the money, and—"

"I remember. I'm fine." I tear off a piece of bagel. Mom is definitely overconcerned. I knew she didn't think I could handle everything that's going on.

"You know we're always here for you and whatever

you need, therapy or whatever, we'll get it." Mom puts her sunglasses on top of her head.

I pause before we get to a place where my teammates could overhear. "I'm not upset about what you said about the therapist. I mean, my medication is covered by insurance, right?"

"Right."

"Okay, so I don't need anything else for my anxiety right now." I shrug. "I have my sketchbook and the breathing exercises and my medication, so what you said about the therapist wasn't a big deal. What made me upset was the swim team thing."

Mom shuffles her feet a bit. "Yeah, we're just looking around at options, honey. Nothing to worry about."

I don't entirely believe her, and her comment about not worrying annoys me. "I just want this year to be fun and normal. Next year will be all serious with high school sports and stuff."

Mom sighs. "Right. Of course. I know there will be more pressure next year, so this year should be fun. Okay. We'll make it through the summer."

"Promise?"

"I promise. As long as things keep looking up, we'll get through the season." Mom puts on her firm face.

That doesn't really sound like a promise to me, but Nico and the other boys are back under our tent and I really want to go. "Okay. I gotta go."

"Okay, hon, good luck in your next race. I'll be

watching!" Mom covers her eyes with her sunglasses and backs away toward the scoring booth.

I wave and head back to the 13–14 tent. I'm glad I didn't tell Mom about Lucas. Then she would really be hovering.

"Dude, I want a bagel!" Owen says when I get back to the tent.

"Better hurry—they're almost out. Burger time coming up." I sit back on my blanket and munch on my second breakfast.

Owen stares at my bagel. "Mmm. Maybe I'll wait for burgers. I love burgers. Or maybe I should get a burger *in* a bagel."

"Dude, you have the best ideas!" Aidan says, rifling through his bag. "Look! Mom packed Cheetos!"

"Score!" Owen grabs the bag and can no longer pay attention to any humans.

But then Ez reaches for the bag. "Now you can pay me back for eating all my chips."

As they scuffle over the snack, Nico leans over to me. "They eat all the time, don't they?"

Owen throws a Cheeto at him. "Hey, we're growing."

I grin. "Swimming burns a lot of calories."

"I guess." Nico is quiet for a minute. I think he's staring at Ez.

"She doesn't have cancer," I say quietly. She's just far enough not to hear us.

"Well, obviously," he says. "I mean, I don't think

people going through chemotherapy can win a race like that."

"Oh." I'm a little embarrassed that I made that assumption. "It's just, a lot of people think that."

"No, I know what cancer looks like. I was actually just looking at her shoulders." Nico lifts his shirt sleeve to reveal a skinny bicep. "She could probably beat me in a bench press in like five seconds. She could probably beat me in anything in five seconds."

"She probably could," I agree. "She's hella strong. She just has alopecia."

"Yeah, Aidan told me." He picks a blade of grass.

Something he said makes me pause. "Wait, so how do you know what cancer looks like?"

"Oh. My grandma had breast cancer a few years ago. She's fine now."

"Oh my god, I'm so sorry." Now I really feel bad for making assumptions.

"It's okay, she's okay now." He stops picking grass and looks at me with those soft brown eyes. "I don't remember it that well, but I do know she did not look like your friend there when she had cancer."

"Wow. Um, I'm glad she's better." Now I also feel bad for thinking how nice his eyes are when he's talking about something serious.

Over the loudspeaker, we hear the announcement calling 13–14 backstroke to the ready bench.

"How come you're not getting up?" Nico asks.

"I'm not doing back today. Lexi knows it's not my

favorite, so she doesn't make me swim it most of the time," I tell him. "I've never really liked not being able to see where I'm going." I'm not sure why I add that last part; it's kind of personal. But it's true.

"Makes sense. So, if backstroke is your least favorite, what is your favorite stroke?" Nico's eyes sparkle. "Not that I really know much about the strokes."

"Well, I've been swimming my entire life, so if you want to learn, you know who to ask." I smile. "And my favorite is probably breaststroke. It has this sort of rhythm to it, you know, like you have to move your arms and your legs independently but in sync with each other. It's hard to learn, but when you get it down and do it long enough, it's soothing. Butterfly is like that, too, I guess, with the rhythm, it's just . . . louder."

I suddenly feel like I'm being overly chatty again. I don't know if that means being nervously chatty is a new symptom of my anxiety, or if I just like talking to Nico.

Nico looks at me like he's actually listening. "You talk about swimming like it's some kind of art or something."

"Yeah, kind of. Art has a rhythm too." I think I'm feeling okay about being chatty. "So, what else do you want to know about swimming?"

"Hmm . . ." He scratches his chin ironically. "Tell me what exactly is happening here today. It's a meet, and you're competing, but you don't have to do every race? How does that work?"

"You've never been to a swim meet before, have you?" I tease.

"Never. Tell me everything. Like, is your age group 13–14, but the next one is 15–18?"

I nod. "Yeah, because there are fewer of us as we get older. Kids do other stuff, high school, you know. There are so few 15–18s they only take up two lanes at practice."

"Got it. Okay. Tell me more."

I'm explaining the order of events to Nico—medley relay, butterfly, backstroke, IM (individual medley—one lap of each stroke), breaststroke, freestyle, free relay, how most of our events are two laps, which is 50 yards, except the IM (which is four laps and so 100 yards), and how we usually only swim three events and one relay per meet—when Sophie comes running back to our tent.

"Hey!" Sophie hollers. "Where's Char? She's supposed to be at the ready bench for back."

I hop up. "I'll find her. Go back to the bench. Sorry," I tell Nico. "Gotta go, teammate duty calls."

He waves me off, and I rush to where I last saw Charlotte: making a TikTok under a tree. She's not there, but I hear a familiar peal of laughter coming from the 15–18 tent. I rush over to find Charlotte and her non-swim team friend Tina laughing hysterically at one of the fifteen-year-old boys. Tina comes to a lot of the meets even though she doesn't swim. And Charlotte loves to hang out with the older kids.

"Char!" I yell. "Ready bench! Now!"

She looks around at the 15–18 girls getting their

things to go to the ready bench. They swim after the 13–14s. "Oh, crap. Help me get my stuff."

"Yep, on it." I hop over to the 13–14 area and grab her cap and goggles while Charlotte pulls off her shorts and bunches up her hair. I follow her to the ready bench and help her get her cap on. She makes it just in time to line up at the blocks behind the last heat of 11–12 boys.

But not before her parents, both of them fuming at the blocks, berate her for not being ready for her race. I think my parents worry too much about me, but Charlotte's parents are always on top of her to get her swimming perfect. It's got to be suffocating.

"Charlotte Ann!" Her mom gets in Charlotte's face as Charlotte stretches her arms. "Where were you?"

"There are scouts here from Tomlin," Charlotte's dad hisses.

"No, there aren't," Charlotte says. "They didn't come. Maybe they're at someone else's meet. I already asked Ez, and she didn't see any either."

I didn't realize Ez had been looking for scouts, but since you never know when they're going to show up, I guess Ez is always looking for them. I feel bad for Charlotte though. She's clearly upset as she hops in the water and reaches for the block to get in place for the backstroke start.

I slip away from Charlotte's parents to watch the race on the side of the pool. "You got this, Char!" I holler and clap. And because Jess is standing next to me, I also holler, "Go Sophie! Go Eels!"

It's a bad race for Charlotte. Back isn't her best stroke, but she's used to winning things. She comes in third, after Sophie and Daniella from River Oaks.

Third is good. She still gets points for the team, but I watch her parents hover and scold her as she climbs out of the pool.

When I get back to our tents to get ready for my breaststroke race, I peek into the 15–18 tent where Charlotte was hanging out just before her almost-missed race. There are a couple of kids in the tent from the other team. By the time swimmers get to 15–18s, they know a lot of the competition from school or other places, or just from years of racing together.

I start to walk away, but I see a familiar flop of bleached blond hair, and I know it's Lucas.

My stomach turns over. Why won't he just stay in his own team's tent? Why does he have to sit there chatting with my team like he's friends with us?

But it gets worse. When Lucas sees me, he hops off his seat and rushes out of the tent. "Maddie!" he calls.

I stop. I want to find out whether he was away at the retreat when the vandalism happened, but I do not want to talk to him. His breath smells like hot dogs, and he makes my skin itch.

"You know I didn't mean anything bad last night, right? In the messages?" Lucas leans in close.

I instinctively pull back. "You mean when you called me self-centered?"

He looks down. "Yeah, I was just sad that you thought I would, like, mess up your pool."

I ignore the fake-hurt in his voice and get to the point. "I heard you got to the retreat late."

"Um, what? The retreat?" Lucas shifts his eyes. "Yeah, I had an ortho appointment, and my brother brought me out to the resort later."

"I didn't know you had a brother." I'm skeptical that Lucas tells the truth about anything.

"Half brother. Like way older from my dad's first wife. He just moved back 'cause he got a fancy new sports business degree and now has a fancy new job at some fancy gym." Lucas rolls his eyes.

"Oh. Okay." I consider that Lucas might be telling the truth about his brother, but that doesn't mean he's telling the truth about when he got to the retreat. "So, you were at the retreat when you posted the picture, but you were still in town when the vandalism happened?"

"I can't believe you would think I put poo and stuff in your pool, Maddie. I would never. We're friends, right? I was just mad that you thought I would lie to you. You should know me better than that." He shakes his head.

"Okay. So, when did you get to the retreat?" I fold my arms over my chest.

"What is this, Twenty Questions? I didn't vandalize your pool, Maddie." Lucas puts his hand over his heart like he's wounded. "I care about you so much. It hurts my feelings that you would think I could ever do that."

And now Lucas is in creepy mode, and somehow I'm the bad guy for asking questions.

"Whatever, I have to go," I mumble. I would so much rather be talking to Nico right now. I hope he hasn't left yet.

"Okay. I'll message you later!" Lucas says, and then he tries to hug me. He puts his arms around my shoulders, but I stiffen. I'm suddenly very aware of how bare my skin is—I'm only wearing a thin pair of shorts over my racing suit.

I drop out of his hug and hurry toward Ez and my friends. I really hope he doesn't message me later, or ever. My shoulders sting from where he touched me. It's not like when my friends hug me. And I know, because some of them, like Aidan, are big huggers.

But when Aidan hugs me, it's because we're friends and he's happy to see me. When Lucas hugs me, it's like he wants something from me.

As I shake off my shoulders, I realize that Lucas never answered my question. He never said when exactly he got to the retreat.

Which means he still might be the East Valley Vandal.

The meet finishes smoothly. We win by a solid twenty points, and both Ez and I feel good about the rest of our races. I see Nico one more time when we cheer on Owen and Aidan swimming the free relay. There's so much chaos at the end of the meet, I can only wave goodbye to him from a distance, but I'm sure I'll see him again.

While Lexi and I help take down the pop-ups with some of the older kids, Mom chats with the River Oaks coach about small businesses in the summer.

"Did that guy from FitWest call you too?" the River Oaks coach asks her.

Mom looks surprised. "He did. Is he making the rounds?"

"Looks like it," the coach says. "He's persistent. But we're not interested."

"No," Mom says. "We aren't either." But she doesn't say that like she's sure of it. It makes me wonder. The FitWest company is persistent with the swim clubs, so FitWest must be pretty eager to buy them up. What would they do to encourage clubs sell to them? Make things difficult for the club?

Would a company like FitWest actually sabotage a swim club with something childish like egging and ketchup pranks to make business difficult and get them to sell?

I don't know if an actual business would sink that low, but if I can't prove Lucas is our vandal, it might be time to investigate FitWest.

Chapter 8

Sunday afternoon, I'm lying on my bed playing on my phone. Sundays are recovery days. The pool is open, but I don't go to it. Saturday meets wear me out. This one more than usual, with everything going on with Lucas that I wish wasn't going on, and everything going on with Nico, which I would like more of.

As I scroll through my feeds, an ad pops up for FitWest gyms. I click on it, and a line catches my eye: *New locations coming soon!* What new locations? Is FitWest so sure they'll buy the local pools that they're advertising new locations already?

I click through to the website and investigate. They already have locations all over California, but the closest one to East Valley pool is across town, which is probably why they're so eager to get a gym out here. They don't have one in this part of the county.

I look through the rest of the pages and land on the one about "Our Team." There's a handful of personal trainers, some salespeople, and a couple of old guys who look like they're in charge. One of the younger sales-people, Derek Bryce, is listed as the "Valley sales rep."

Derek *Bryce*? Like Lucas's older brother with the

fancy new gym job? That's who's trying to buy our club and River Oaks too? My heart races. Why do there have to be more Bryces in my life?

Mom and Dad don't know anything about Lucas. I mean, for two years he was just this annoying guy at school crushing on me and messaging me too much. There wasn't much to say. What would they think if I told them their sales rep is related to the kid I think might be responsible for the vandalism at our pool?

I think they would be mad. I think they would wonder why I didn't tell them sooner, and then they would freak out about how this is going to trigger my anxiety. Which—newsflash—it already has, and I'm handling it.

But my parents would probably think I wasn't.

When I look up Derek's Instagram account, he's got all these arty pics of clubs and pools in the city with captions like *Check out this gem!* and *This one has old-school appeal, but wait until we add FitWest machines for a new level of fitness!* It's so cringey. But his posts have tons of likes, and he has a lot of followers. Enough that he probably thinks people want him to buy all these pools and clubs and turn them into gyms.

He also has a picture of himself with Lucas. They're at one of the FitWest gyms next to some weight machines. It's hashtagged #littlebro.

I don't know why guys have to take pictures of themselves all sweaty, but an idea forms in my head. Maybe Lucas's big brother is working with him to vandalize our pool so we have to cancel practices and lose business. Because it's the lost business following the vandalism that's making my parents consider selling the club. Anger surges through me. I'm sure Derek Bryce wants us to have lots of bad business days.

I keep scrolling through Derek's Instagram for more info and land on a picture of our pool. The post is dated June 12, but I have no idea when he actually took the picture, because the pool is completely empty. Could he have snuck in when we weren't open? A shiver runs down my spine.

It's a beautiful shot of our pool without lane lines, filtered to make it look like mist is rising around it. The caption reads *Can you see yourself taking a FitWest aqua class here? I can!* My stomach turns over. He really wants to turn our club into a gym.

Worse, the comments. A bunch of people have posted the hands-raised emoji or little things like *great pool!* But one comment really riles me. It's posted by someone named @KarenA456. She says, *would love FW to run East Valley! Great pool but always so many kids in it.*

So much for my relaxing, worry-free Sunday. I feel like I have to tell someone about the picture though. It means Derek the FitWest guy was at our pool when it wasn't open.

And if he knows how to take pictures of the pool when it's not open, could he and his #littlebro also be vandalizing our pool when it's not open? My blood boils.

I have to show my parents. Mom's at the club

teaching her Gentle Yoga class, so I storm downstairs to show my dad Derek's Instagram. But I find my brother in the kitchen instead.

"Dude, what are you doing here?" I blurt.

"Uh, I live here." Jack shoves a giant piece of pizza in his mouth.

"No, I mean, why aren't you working? You're supposed to be working today, right?"

"Yeah, I just came home for lunch. So tired of snack bar food."

"I can't believe you're tired of any food," I say. My brother hasn't stopped eating in four years.

"True, I am a growing boy." Jack grins a mouthful of crust and flexes his muscles.

"Ew. Whatever. So, who's on the guard chair right now?"

"Lex," Jack says between chewing.

"And who else?"

"Just Lex. It was slow."

My heart sinks. "Slow? Why?"

"Dude, Mad, don't worry. Sunday afternoons are always slow. It'll pick up in the evening," Jack attempts to reassure me.

"I guess."

"Hey, you know who is there today?" Jack mumbles while shoving another slice of pizza in his mouth. "That guy you like, the one who hangs out with Owen Wu and Aidan."

"What guy?" I know he's talking about Nico, but I didn't know that he knew about Nico.

"You know, the new guy. If you like him, you should get over to the pool, 'cause girls in this town love new guys and someone's gonna be all over him in like two seconds."

I punch his arm. "I thought all the girls in town were in love with you."

"Well, obviously. But there's only so much of me to go around." Jack does a little shimmy dance.

"Gross. And what do you mean, 'that guy I like'? What makes you think I like this new guy anyway?" I've only talked to Nico twice.

Jack talks through bites. "Well, 'cause you were chatting him up last week at the pool, and then at the meet you could not stop staring at him."

I didn't know anyone had seen me talking to Nico, but if I had to choose, I'd rather my family see me talking to him than to Lucas. "Dude, you weren't even at the meet very long."

"Uh-uh, little sis. I was at the meet long enough. I didn't leave to do the lifeguard shift until after the IMs. You just didn't notice, 'cause you were too busy paying attention to new guy."

He's right. I didn't even watch my own brother in his races. "Oh. Sorry. And um, he has a name. Nico."

"I knew it! I knew you like him!" Jack accuses. "And it's fine. I didn't watch all of your races either."

"Um . . . I don't think knowing his name means I

like him." Jack's right though—I think I do like him. Because I do not like thinking of him at the pool talking to other girls.

"A brother knows these things!" Jack stands and brushes pizza crumbs off his face. "I gotta go back to work. You coming so you can get your man?"

I'm torn. I want to be around Nico, but I'm not up for the pool today. Meets take so much out of me. "No. I just—"

"I know. Recovery day." He puts a hand on my shoulder.

"Yeah. Plus, I have to talk to Dad about something. Seen him?"

"Yep." He points to the backyard.

"K. Thanks. Have fun with all the pool girls." I give his shoulder a nudge.

Jack puffs up his chest. "I will distract all the ladies so they pay no attention to your new guy. Except for the ladies whose tastes run more toward our beautiful sister. I have no power over them."

I have to laugh. "Thanks, bro."

"I do this for you, Mad! It's a tough job, but someone has to be the hottest guy in the neighborhood." Jack puts a fist to his chest. "You're lucky I'm so willing to offer my services."

I roll my eyes and head into the backyard, trying to shake off the image of Nico talking to a bunch of girls. Dad's in a straw hat and shorts, pulling weeds from his small vegetable garden.

"Hey, hon!" Dad hollers when I slam the back door.

"Hey." I sit on the edge of a planter box. "Can you look at this for a sec?"

Dad brushes his dirty hands on his ragged shorts. "Sure, what's up?"

I show him my phone. "This guy, Derek, he posted this picture of the pool, *our* pool, on Instagram. It seems weird because the pool is empty. I think it looks like he must have snuck in or something." I show Dad the pic of the pool and a few that show Derek's face.

"What?" Dad looks closer. "Nah, that Derek guy, I met him. He's the FitWest guy. He came to the pool one day when you all were still in school and gave me the whole spiel about how he can help us out. But really he wants to buy the club." Dad yanks a weed from the box. "He must have taken some pictures while he was there. I think I was the only one out at the pool. Mom was doing her yoga class in the clubhouse."

I look at the pool again. "You don't think it seems weird? I mean, the pool looks empty."

Dad shrugs and digs around for more weeds. "I think he's just a sales guy. Checking stuff out, you know how it is. Hey, would you mind grabbing me a bottle of water when you go back in? It's getting warm out here."

"Wait, look, there's something else," I say. I pull up the photo Lucas posted the day of the vandalism. I don't want to tell my dad that Lucas has been bothering me, but I can tell my dad that Lucas is posting mean stuff about us. "This is what Derek's little brother posted. He goes to my school. They're out to get us, Dad."

Dad looks at the picture. "Don't all thirteen-year-old boys take any excuse to talk about bathroom humor?"

I pause. "Um, not really?" I don't think I've ever heard Aidan and Owen talk about poop.

Dad chuckles. "I think they just don't talk about it around girls! But they still talk about it."

I'm not really finding this funny. I pocket my phone. Dad is clearly not receptive to the possibility that Derek and/or Lucas Bryce are behind the recent incidents at the pool.

"Yeah, okay." I pass my easel that's set up in the backyard for painting and head back into the house.

"Oh, and Maddie?" Dad calls.

"Yeah?" I pause.

"Why are you looking around at the FitWest guy's social media anyway? You don't need to worry about that. I told him we didn't want to sell."

There it is. I knew if I brought it up, someone would tell me not to worry. I'm glad I didn't say anything about Lucas's crush. Dad would definitely think I didn't have my anxiety under control if he knew I thought Lucas was specifically targeting me.

"Okay. I was just curious. I'll forget it." But I'm not going to forget it. I double-check the date on the pic of the empty pool. It was the last day of school. The day practice got canceled because of glass. Maybe Derek really did come and talk to Dad that day or that week.

Or maybe one of the Bryce brothers snuck into the pool to take a picture and brought some broken glass with him.

I'm more convinced than ever that Lucas is our East Valley Vandal. Only now I think he has the help of his older brother.

Chapter 9

I can't get Derek the FitWest guy or his #littlebro Lucas out of my head. I check both of their Instagrams every day. Derek hasn't posted anything else about pools or clubs, just selfies of himself working out. Gross. And Lucas has only posted pics of him and his River Oaks swim friends doing ridiculous jumps off the blocks.

I don't like looking at Lucas's Instagram, but it's necessary research. I can't help but worry that unless we find out who vandalized our pool and get them to stop, something else is going to happen. Something worse.

Tuesday morning, we're all hanging out in the locker room after practice, chatting and talking about the next meet. It's Saturday against South Hills. They're a pretty small team and we usually beat them, but it's a good opportunity to break personal records and try strokes that we don't usually swim. Lexi is even making me swim backstroke.

As we all change into clothes to go home, Charlotte pulls a razor and a shiny pink-capped bottle of shaving cream out of her bag and turns on the shower.

Sophie yanks a T-shirt over her head. "Why shave

now?" she asks Charlotte. "Don't you wait until Friday night, so you're smooth for the meet?"

Most of the swim team girls who shave their legs go the whole week without shaving and then do it right before the meet. They say the smoothness helps them feel more aerodynamic. I wouldn't know, because I don't shave my legs.

"I'm always smooth for the meet!" Ez runs a hand over her hairless arms. "Low maintenance hair care—thank you, alopecia!"

Everyone laughs, even though we've heard Ez say that before. But because Ez and I tell each other everything, I know that sometimes she'll shave if she gets a little patch of hair on part of her head or part of her body. Alopecia is unpredictable that way.

Charlotte pops the cap off her shaving cream. "I'm shaving now 'cause I don't have time before Tyler's swim party later," she says. "I'm meeting Tina for breakfast, then we're going to the mall and straight from there to Tyler's."

"Tyler? Like Tyler on our team, Tyler?" Jess asks as she sits on the bench next to Sophie.

"Yeah, that Tyler." Charlotte smears pink-tinted shaving cream on her left leg. "He invited us on Saturday, and I am not going to my first swim party at a freshman's house with hairy legs."

"Isn't he kind of old for you?" Ez looks up from her bag. "High school?"

"Old for what?" Charlotte smiles slyly. "It's just a

swim party. Plus, he's only fourteen. He's still in our age group. And yeah, he'll be a freshman in the fall, but we'll be eighth graders—it's not that different."

"But a freshman at a different school, right?" I say. "I mean, since you'll probably go to Tomlin and Tyler goes to East Valley?" Most of the high school kids on the team go to East Valley High, the public high school. It's where Jack goes and where Lexi went and where I'll go.

Charlotte shrugs like she didn't hear my question. "Hey, you want to come to the party, Maddie? Except Lucas is going to be there, and I know you don't like him. But it wouldn't kill you to be nice to him, you know."

Ez grumbles from the bench. "She is already too nice to him."

"No, thank you," I tell Charlotte.

Sophie smiles knowingly and nudges my shoulder. "Because you like Aidan's cousin, huh?"

My skin gets tingly. "Um, I didn't like Lucas before I even met Aidan's cousin, so no, I just don't like Lucas. It has nothing to do with anyone else."

"Okay, well, you don't have to be so mean about it. I was just asking," Charlotte says as she slides the razor over her leg. I shiver noticeably. "Anyway, Maddie, when are you gonna start shaving?" she asks without looking up from her work.

"Never."

Charlotte rinses her razor in the shower. "At least you have light leg hair and it's not that obvious."

That's not why I don't shave my legs. I don't shave

because the idea of a razor all over my body makes my skin crawl. Thank you, anxiety-related sensory issues.

But I'm not the only one not shaving my legs. Lots of girls my age don't shave their legs.

Jess pipes up. "Aw, leave Maddie alone. I literally only shave for meets. Saves me time and it's environmentally friendly. So, good on you, Mad."

Sophie puts her arm around Jess. "And I think you're hot, so I guess it's working!"

Charlotte rolls her eyes and slathers her right leg with shaving cream. "Whatever. I'm not waiting to shave until just before a meet. There are too many hot guys around this pool."

Her comment makes me wonder if she thinks Nico is one of them. I hope not.

"And we all know hot guys love a hairless girl, right?" Ez grins and makes everyone laugh.

"Ow!" Charlotte winces dramatically.

"Cut yourself?" Sophie acts mildly concerned.

"No, I just forgot my puppy scratched me last night when he thought my flip-flops were attacking him," Charlotte explains. "And this stuff stings in open cuts."

"I didn't know you had a puppy," I say, hoping we can switch the conversation away from shaving. Just talking about it makes me queasy.

"Yeah. My brother's the one who wanted to get him, but my parents somehow think taking care of a puppy would give me more responsibility and help me prepare for high school or something. Like I need more things to be responsible about," she groans.

As Charlotte rinses her legs in the shower, the shaving cream bottle slips out of her hands and hits the floor with a clang. "Oops!" she giggles.

My heart suddenly races. "Tell me you didn't chip the tile."

Charlotte looks down. "Nope, no chips, just a slightly dented bottle. I mean, no chips that weren't already here."

I didn't realize the chipped tile was so obvious to people outside my family. I wonder if there's a certain number of chipped tiles you can have to pass inspection.

After everyone leaves the locker room, I check the spot where Charlotte dropped her shaving cream. There isn't a chip—she was right about that—but I spot what looks like a hair running through the faded green tile. I try to wipe the hair away, but it turns out it's not a hair.

It's a crack. A small one, but small cracks get bigger and turn into chips. I hope my parents don't notice. It might just push them over the edge and make them want to sell this club immediately.

When I leave the locker room, Ez is waiting on the pool deck, sporting her floppy hat and watching the next age group practice. We were in the locker room for a while. The 11–12s and 9–10s are through with their warm-ups.

Lexi waves us over. "Maddie! Ezzie! Come here."

"What's up?" I ask. Ez pulls down the brim of her floppy hat. The sun is already beating on the concrete pavement.

"Are you two free later this morning?" Lexi doesn't take her eyes off her swimmers while she talks to us. I hope she's not going to ask me something about the vandalism or Lucas, or tell me not to worry about something. Or everything.

"Yeah, I gotta eat breakfast, but after that I'm good," I say.

"Same." Ez nods.

"Good. Hang on—Carson, keep your feet together in a butterfly kick!" Lexi hollers toward the water. Carson gives her a thumbs-up and keeps his feet together. "So, next hour I'm going to attempt to teach the 6-and-unders breaststroke. Can you two get in the water and help me out? You know how hard it is to get the rhythm without a person right there."

"Yeah, totally!" Ez says. She loves sharing her joy of swimming.

"Sure. What's in it for us?" I raise my eyebrows, relieved that Lexi's request is fun and productive and has nothing to do with vandalism.

"Really?" Lexi grins. "Your friend will help me for free, but my own family wants something from me?"

"I mean, this is *your* job." I snicker.

"Fine." Lexi shakes her head. "Carson! Feet together! All right. Kari's stopping by this afternoon. I'll have her pick up some fancy iced coffees for you two."

"Deal!" Ez bounces.

"You were going to do it even without the iced coffees!" I bump Ez's shoulder. "But fine, we'll do it. Since you have a nice girlfriend who gets us treats."

Lexi smiles. "I do have good taste in girlfriends. Thanks, you two."

I check the clock over the blocks. Nine fifteen. During the week, we swim from seven thirty to nine, the middle groups swim from nine to ten, and the little ones go from ten to ten forty-five. Then the pool opens for rec swim at eleven sharp. "Okay. See you in forty-five minutes."

Ez and I are still laughing about Lexi's iced-coffee bribery when we head out the pool gates. But my easy laughs turn to nervous giggles when I see who's in the parking lot.

Owen and Aidan sit on their bikes, wet hair tousled. Joining them on a third bike but without the wet hair is Nico.

Ez grabs my arm. "Ooh, check out the cute-boy bike brigade."

I guess Owen and Aidan are cute, but I've known them too long to really think about them that way. Nico definitely is. He's wearing sneakers and crisp new shorts and a faded purple T-shirt that says Vikings on it. He's already smiling because he's talking to his friends, but I'm pretty sure his smile widens when he sees me.

"Hi, Maddie." Nico pushes his hair back from his cute face.

"Hi," I stammer.

Owen responds by popping a wheelie and yelling, "Heeellllooo, ladies!"

Ez hollers, "Is that the best you can do?"

"Oh, you think we are athletic gods in the pool? Well, you haven't seen the bike stylings of Wu, James, and Marquez yet!" Owen calls as he catches his balance.

Nico stops his bike next to me. "There are no bike stylings of Wu, James, and Marquez. I have no idea what he's talking about."

I giggle and wonder if I'm blushing.

Aidan circles the parking lot. "We're just running security out here. Gotta keep away all the evil vandals and protect our favorite pool."

"I'm sure the evil vandals will be very intimidated by your bike skills." Ez laughs.

Nico leans close to my ear. "Everything's okay, right?"

"Yeah, no more condiments on the pool deck." I don't know if that means it's okay though. My stomach has been in knots every morning this week, and I'm always hoping I don't walk through the pool gate to find another mess, or Lexi injured on the ground, or something worse.

"Hey, do they know who did it yet?" Owen shouts while pedaling.

I shake my head. "Still no one really trying to find out." Except me and Ez, I think. "My dad keeps saying it was a prank."

"Nasty prank," Owen says. "We'll keep an eye out though, Mad—Wu, James, and Marquez to the rescue!"

I can't help but laugh. "Just don't hurt yourselves."

"Hey, Maddie!" Aidan yells, even though he's like two feet away.

"Standing right here, A." I smile.

"Sorry, I just got excited." Aidan lowers his voice. "So, what's up with Lucas Bryce being all weird with you at the River Oaks meet?"

My heart skips. I was hoping no one saw me talking to Lucas. I was hoping no one knew that I ever talked to Lucas. "Um, what do you mean?"

"Dude, he hugged you, and you, like, turned into a zombie." Aidan spins the wheel on his bike.

"Yeah, uh, he's not super good at getting messages," I mumble. I don't really know what to say. Especially since Nico is looking at me like he's very curious about someone seen hugging me.

Ez comes to my rescue. "He wants to get out of Maddie's friend zone." She puts her hands on her hips. "But Maddie is not interested."

I nod. "Yes, exactly that, thank you. I am not interested in Lucas. At all." I might be imagining it, but I think I see a look of relief cross Nico's face.

Aidan can't stop circling his bike. "What does that even mean, friend zone? And why is it bad? I think a friend zone sounds awesome. Like, can we be in a friend zone? Like, this curb here says 'loading zone,' so this must be a zone here at this pool, and we're all friends?"

Ez tries to grab his handlebars as he circles. "We already are! You didn't get the memo that this here is the East Valley Friend Zone?"

Aidan pulls his bike right up to Ez. "Awesome! I love friends!"

Owen pulls his bike next to Aidan's. "So, are there rules to this friend zone? Boundaries? Explain."

"No rules, no limits, no dress code!" Aidan hollers.

"Well, maybe a little dress code." Ez laughs. "Like, you have to be dressed. Swimsuits are an acceptable form of being dressed."

Aidan winks. It's cheesy, but it's Aidan, so cheesy is endearing. "Agreed. Hair is optional, clothing is not."

Ez glows. "Perfect. I'm in."

Aidan puts his feet back on his pedals. "So, Friend Zone, we're getting breakfast—you want to come? You can ride on my handlebars."

Ez laughs again. "Sounds tempting, but broken bones will really slow down my times, so I think I'll pass on the handlebar ride."

Nico looks at me. "Really, you two want to come? We can ride slow or ditch the bikes or whatever."

I do want to, but I look at my watch. Nine twenty. Not enough time. "Oh, we would, but my sister just asked us to help her with the sixers at ten."

Owen pops another wheelie over a parking curb. "Tell her you have plans!"

I glance at Ez, who smiles but shakes her head. "Next time?" I ask.

"Okay." Nico looks disappointed, which is very cute.

"Fine!" Owen hollers as he rides down the street. "Next time you better!"

Ez and I both giggle as we watch the boys ride off. My heart is close to bursting. We've gone to breakfast with Owen and Aidan after practice before, but usually with the team. And never with someone like Nico. It feels different. I think Ez feels it too.

I'm about to ask her if she might be crushing on one of the boys when Nico peels away from the other two and bikes back to us.

I grab Ez's arm. "Oh my god, he's coming back."

"Girl! Chill!" she whispers, but I can hear the smile in her voice.

"Hey, Maddie!" Nico calls as he stops his bike next to us. "Um, Aidan wouldn't give me your number. He said if I want to text you, I have to ask you for it myself. Something about how he doesn't want dudes messaging you if you don't want them to, because that is not a friendly thing to do. He might actually have said 'a friend-zonely thing to do,' but I don't think that's a word."

I giggle. "Yeah, that sounds like Aidan. But okay." I pull out my phone and my heart flutters. "So, um, put your number in my phone, and I'll text you."

Next to me, Ez tries to contain her excitement as Nico punches his number into my phone. "Sweet. Text me later?" he says.

"Okay." I can't help but grin. It seems I do a lot of grinning when Nico is around.

"Bye, Maddie," he sings as he pedals away.

Ez and I wait until the boys are out of view before jumping and squealing. "Okay, dang Mad, he is cute!"

"I know, right?" I stare at his phone number on my phone. "Like, really cute."

"He likes you." She nudges my shoulder.

"Well, it's just a number." I'm trying not to get too excited. "I mean, I've had Owen's and Aidan's numbers forever."

"Um, whatever. I don't think Nico's asking other girls for their numbers." She bumps my hip as we walk down the street.

I stare at my phone, trying to decide if I should text Nico now or later when I realize the time on it. Nine thirty-two.

"Oh crap, we gotta be back at the pool in less than a half hour," I say as we stop in front of Ez's house.

"I almost forgot!" Ez takes her hat off to go into her house. "Okay, I'm just gonna grab food and change into my other suit. Meet you back here in twenty?"

"You got it!" I run to my house to get ready.

But it feels more like flying.

Chapter 10

I text Nico that afternoon, and we text back and forth all week. He tells me he can't come to the meet on Saturday at South Hills because he and his mom are still unpacking and she's making him go furniture shopping.

But he wants me to text him after the meet, so on Sunday afternoon while I lie on my bed and recover, I pull out my phone and text him.

> Me: hey

Nico responds right away.

> Nico: hey

> Me: what r u doing?

> Nico: painting my bedroom

> Me: impressive

> Nico: eh it's not a very big bedroom

> how was the meet?

> A says you won

Me: yeah, the team won

i did ok

but i had to swim backstroke

Nico: sorry did it go ok?

Me: ok for backstroke

Nico: cool i have paint all over my hands

Me: k maybe you should get back to painting then

Nico: what r u doing this week?

Me: swimming

Nico: want to hang out?

Me: ok

Nico: i have to help mom with house stuff maybe wednesday we can come to pool?

Me: bring a suit this time 😊

I'm giddy with the idea of seeing Nico again. It's at the pool, so it's not like a date, I guess, but it's planned, which seems like kind of a big deal. I text Ez with a re-hash of the conversation. I wonder if I should also tell my parents. Or ask Lexi for advice. Or maybe warn Jack so he doesn't do anything embarrassing.

Or maybe I'll just pretend I'm going to the pool on

Wednesday like normal and hope no one notices anything is different. Even if I know it is.

Tuesday night, just as I put my phone away to go to bed, I notice a new notification. I think it's another text from Nico about hanging out tomorrow, and a smile twitches my lips. But it's not Nico; it's Lucas with an Instagram message.

Lucas: my parents are getting a divorce

I don't really know how to respond to that. I don't want to respond to that at all. Why is he even telling me? Maybe if I keep it nice and short, he'll go away.

Me: sorry

Lucas: i just wanted to talk to someone about it

Me: ok

Lucas: it sucks

Me: yeah

Lucas: will you go out wi me?

im sad I need something to be happy about

Me: sorry

Lucas: please i would be a good
     boyfriend but nobody ever sees how
     good a boyfriend i would be

I don't think Lucas would be a good boyfriend. Mostly because I'm not attracted to him. But also because he doesn't really pick up on hints like when someone doesn't want to be hugged or doesn't want to go out with him.

Me: i think you need to focus on
     yourself right now.

Lucas: is that a no are you telling me
     no

Me: i am

Lucas: if you say no I don't know what
     ill do

What does that mean? It sounds like a threat. Like he doesn't know if he'll vandalize my pool?

I can't figure out what to say next. I start to write a bunch of messages and they all sound either too mean or too soft, where he might think I like him. I wonder if I should tell someone. But I can't tell my parents and make them think I can't handle things myself. Finally, I just text Lucas *I have to go to bed*, and then I turn off my phone completely.

But I can't sleep. I don't understand what Lucas meant by "I don't know what I'll do." I think he just said that to make me feel sorry for him, but I can't stop thinking about the smashed snow globe and the vandalism at our pool and the things Lucas could do.

When I wake up for practice Wednesday morning, there are no new messages. I check Lucas's Instagram, and there's a picture of him at the River Oaks pool dressed in sweats with a caption saying *early practice* 😊.

He didn't respond to my last message. Good. I want nothing more to do with him. I don't even want to think about him.

At practice, it feels like it's going to be a perfect day. The air is clear, and it's just warm enough that I know it's going to be hot (like most days in the summer here) but not scorching hot. Perfect weather for hanging out with a guy I actually like, and not thinking about a guy who doesn't understand that I don't like him.

It's also been a couple of weeks since our pool was vandalized. Maybe the police were right—it was all just a couple of dumb pranks.

Between thinking about my sort-of-date with Nico and Lucas's irritating texts, I'm not even thinking about practice. I barely notice when Ez and Charlotte start talking about racing again.

"Let's do it now! Before practice starts." Ez bounces up and down.

"Now?" Charlotte moans. "But we've been racing at meets. Isn't that enough?"

"But we never got our race that day with the glass thing, you know?" Ez sparkles with excitement. "We need a rematch."

Lexi drops a stack of kickboards on the deck with a thud. "You want to race, do it now before practice starts. We've got a ton of work to do today. This is hardcore training week."

The rest of the team groans.

"Ugh, why?" Jess asks from the bench. She looks like she's not quite awake yet.

"No meet coming up because of the holiday," Lexi says. We never have meets on Fourth of July weekend. "So, it's a good week to train hard and build strength with enough time to recover before the next meet. I have a packed workout for you today. You want to race, it's now or never."

I actually don't mind a harder workout today. It'll help me get out any nervous energy before seeing Nico tonight. Ez likes a hard workout too. But she likes racing more.

Ez bounces off her seat. "Yeah, let's do it, Char. Twenty-five free. No breath. Right now."

"Without warming up?" Charlotte asks.

"Yeah, yeah. They do drills like this at Tomlin all the time. No warm-up, straight in the water. They say it keeps you always ready." Ez stretches her arms over her head. "We want to go to Tomlin, we gotta get used to this kind of thing."

"Fine." Charlotte pulls out her cap and goggles. "Let's get it over with."

Charlotte reluctantly sluffs off her sweats and tucks her hair into her cap. A bright-red scratch lines her arm.

"That puppy get you again?" I touch her arm lightly.

"What?" Charlotte yanks her arm back. "Oh. Yeah. I had to take him out this morning. Annoying dog." She takes a while fussing with her goggles, but finally she follows Ez to the blocks.

As she passes Sophie, Ez says, "Time me? I'm going for under fourteen seconds."

Sophie nods and pulls out her phone. Ez is always serious about racing. This isn't just about her beating Charlotte, though she would love that; this is also about beating her own time. Swimming is always a big deal to Ez.

But swimming feels like less and less of a big deal to Charlotte. She glances around the pool deck like she's looking for something—an audience, maybe—then grabs her phone and takes a selfie. For Charlotte, documenting her races feels more important than winning them.

The rest of the team stays on the side of the pool, still in our sweats. Jess lets out a loud yawn, but the rest of us cheer for Ez and Charlotte. I think I even hear Owen and Aidan talk about placing bets. They've declined the invite to join the race this time.

"I'm saving my energy for the hard workout," Owen says with a yawn when I ask him why he's not racing.

"I've actually become mildly terrified of those two together," Aidan whispers. I giggle.

"All right, you two!" Lexi calls, just like she did a few weeks ago when they tried this the first time. Ez places her goggles and climbs on the block. Charlotte gives her adoring fans a thumbs-up and theatrically slides onto the block.

"Swimmers, take your mark," Lexi says. In unison, Charlotte and Ez grip the edges of the blocks. Lexi blows her whistle and Ez fires off the block.

But Charlotte stands up and hops off the block, holding up her goggles. "Strap broke," she says.

But we're not really paying attention to her. Ez hasn't noticed she's racing alone, and the team keeps cheering her on from the sidelines.

Sophie counts the seconds, "Eleven, twelve . . ."

Ez touches the wall right at fourteen.

Cheers erupt from the team when Ez pops her head up. Ez starts to lift her arms in triumph, but a pained look crosses her face, and she drops her arms on the pool deck.

Something's wrong.

Ez pulls herself out of the pool, gasping for breath. A loud, shrieking alarm sounds across the deck. Some kids put their hands over their ears, but nothing can block out that sound.

The cheers turn into panic. My heart pounds against my chest. I try to hurry toward Ez, but Lexi grabs me before I can get to her. "No! Stay away. Get everyone down to the parking lot area. Hurry."

"What?" I feel like I can barely move, let alone get other people to move. It sounds like a fire alarm, but there's no smoke.

Because it's not a fire alarm. It's the chlorine-leak alarm.

Lucas.

He did it. He was mad at me for rejecting him again last night, so he must have come here and caused a chlorine leak. My eyes dart around, looking for a glimpse of him.

Lexi zips around the pool deck. "Jack!" she calls to my brother. I hadn't even seen him yet this morning. "Jack! Turn off the tanks! Cover your mouth!"

Jack pulls off his T-shirt and holds it over his face as he runs to the fenced-in area where the chemicals are stored.

On the edge of the pool, Ez curls into a ball and coughs violently. The alarm still rings, screeching confusion. I can't move. How could Lucas do this to us? I should have just kept the snow globe. Then he wouldn't be so mad.

Lexi grabs one of the boys. "Tyler! Get Ez to the lawn, away from the pool." Finally, she turns to me. "Maddie, what are you doing? I said get everyone down to the parking lot."

I snap into action, grabbing kids and pushing them

toward the exit. But all I can think about is my best friend gasping for air.

And it feels like it's all my fault.

Chapter 11

I manage to find Sophie and Jess and tell them to help me get everyone out. This is different from the time Lucas pulled the alarm at Maple Grove. That time was kind of funny, and no one crawled out of the pool gasping for breath.

This time is not funny at all. It's terrifying.

I can't believe he would do this. I can't believe he would do something that would hurt my best friend. Did he mean for it to hurt me? Or was he just trying to close the pool again? I push those thoughts out of my head and work on making sure everyone is okay.

When I catch sight of Charlotte, she's carefully putting her sweats back on. She moves like she's in a daze, but I don't think Charlotte's been affected by the chlorine leak. The leak hit at the opposite end of the pool, where Ez got out, not the end where Charlotte was standing at the blocks. But Charlotte's eyes are glassy, and her face is gray.

"Are you okay?" I take Charlotte's arm and lead her out to the parking lot.

"Yeah." She stares at the ground. "What happened?" The rest of the team fills the parking lot. They must have left the pool area quickly, while I was trying to get answers from Lexi.

"Chlorine leak." I try to figure out the details. "The tanks are at the end of the pool away from the blocks. Only Ez was over there. Everyone else was closer to the blocks . . . and Ez must have been holding her breath, so when she finished the race, she took such a huge breath that she inhaled chlorine gas."

"Oh my god. Is she going to be okay?" Charlotte twists her towel in her hands.

"I think so." I hear sirens in the distance, coming closer. Lexi must have called 911. The kids huddle in groups and stare at the street. No one knows what to do.

Except maybe my brother. Jack moves through the groups of swimmers, putting a comforting hand on their shoulders and checking to see if they're okay. He even checks the pulse of a couple of kids. I wonder if Lexi told him to do that or if that's just his lifeguard training kicking in.

Before the sirens reach us, my family's familiar blue minivan screeches around the corner and into the parking lot. Mom's driving. She parks illegally, and Dad practically falls out of the front seat.

Dad rushes to me and grabs my face. "You okay?" I nod, and he says, "Stay here." Then he runs through the gate into the pool area.

Mom climbs out of the car, phone to her ear. She hollers at the kids gathered in the parking lot, "Everyone stay here! Don't leave."

"Why can't they leave?" I ask her.

"Ambulance on the way. I want everyone checked," she says. "Dang it, why isn't Maria picking up?"

"Ez's mom? She works so late at the restaurant, she's probably sleeping," I say. Lexi or Jack must have called our parents after Lexi called 911. I can't believe I didn't think to call Ez's mom. Or even my mom.

"You're right. Jack! Take the van, go to Ez's house, and get her mom. Tell her to meet us at the hospital. Drive her there if you have to," Mom orders.

Jack looks up from a group of kids and asks incredulously, "Really?" He's only had his license for about three months.

"Yes. Just go. Tell her that everything is—oh . . ." Mom stops and stares at the gate of the pool. Lexi and Tyler hold Ez between their arms. She's walking with their help, but her eyes keep fluttering. Ez's face is completely pale, and I've never seen her look so weak.

I hurry toward my best friend just as the ambulance pulls in. "Are you—"

But Lexi shakes her head. "Not now. She'll be okay once she gets some air."

The EMTs are on us in seconds. They sit Ez on the back of the ambulance and check her out while they ask Lexi all kinds of questions about what happened. I hover nearby. I don't want to leave Ez, but I don't know what I'm supposed to do.

When they get to the questions about Ez's health, Lexi glances at me. "You know her better than anyone."

"Is she on any medication?" a ponytailed EMT addresses me with gentle eyes.

"Uh, no, she doesn't like to take anything. Even, like, ibuprofen," I tell her.

"She has alopecia, correct?" she asks.

"Yes." I watch another EMT put what I think is an oxygen mask over Ez's face. It looks like something you'd see in a space movie.

"I thought so." The EMT nods. "Okay, thanks. Any other health issues?" A fire truck pulls up behind them.

"I don't think so." I feel like I should say something else about Ez, like how strong she is and how hard she trains. I want them to know how healthy she is, even if she doesn't have hair. But I guess they know about alopecia.

I must look nervous because the EMT looks more closely at my face. "Are you okay?" she asks. "You seem to be having some trouble breathing. Were you near the leak?"

She's right, even though I didn't realize it. My breath feels shallow. "Oh. No. I just—"

Lexi watches me. "She has anxiety. Maddie, go sit down and do your breathing. It's okay."

The EMT touches my arm. "Your friend is going to be okay. I can tell she's healthy, and her coach got her to fresh air in time. You've been very helpful."

I nod at her and do what Lexi tells me. Sitting on the curb, I take a deep breath in and count to five. Then I exhale for five. I do this a few more times, and I feel a tiny bit better.

While I'm sitting on the curb, I try to make sense of the situation. Lexi and Ez are still at the ambulance. The people from the fire truck are checking out the other swimmers. Owen and Aidan; Charlotte, Sophie, Jess—they all get checked out by the fire techs, but they look okay.

Mom comes over to me. "You all right, hon?" she asks, but she's not looking at me. She's watching the other kids.

"Yeah. I'm okay. Is Ez okay?" I watch the EMTs get Ez into the ambulance. She's still in her bathing suit.

"Yep, she's going to be fine." Then Mom motions to Lexi. "Lex, ride in the ambulance with Ezzie."

Lexi nods and climbs in after Ez.

I look up at my mom. "What are you and Dad going to do?"

Mom watches worried parents zip into the parking lot, some in cars, some on foot. I didn't even notice when the other parents started to arrive. Almost all the kids have their phones in their hands.

Mom pulls a hair tie out of her pocket and ties up her hair as she walks toward the parents. "Damage control."

After everyone but one police car has left, Mom and I find my dad on the pool deck.

"Should Dad even be here by the pool?" I ask Mom. "Isn't there still gas around?"

Mom shakes her head. "I think it's okay. It got shut off quick, and the gas will dissipate in the fresh air. A couple of the fire department people checked it out and said it's okay for now, but they'll come back tomorrow to make sure it's okay for swimmers." Mom pauses. "It probably wouldn't have affected Ez so much if she hadn't just finished racing."

"Okay. So why is that police car still here?"

"Just to keep everyone away for a bit," she explains.

Dad is standing in front of the tiny fenced-off area where the chlorine tanks are stored. He's talking to someone on the phone. He touches a knob and then stands back, a frown on his face. He reaches for the alarm but pulls his arm back. It's like he can't figure out what he should do. Dad ends his call and stares at the equipment.

The chlorine tanks are opposite the girls' locker room, backed up against the chain-link fence that separates our club from the small shopping center next door. A wooden fence with a gate blocks the tanks on three sides; the fourth side is blocked by the chain-link fence, covered in thick blackberry bushes. Because of the prickly bushes, it's pretty hard to get to the tanks unless you use the gate, which is latched but not locked.

Dad holds the wooden gate open and inspects the latch and hinges, which are engineered to close automatically unless something is holding them open.

As Mom reaches him, my phone buzzes. It's Lexi.

> **Lexi:** Ez is okay her mom is here and she'll go home today

> tell mom. she didn't answer her phone

> > **Me:** ok thanks

> **Lexi:** Jacks gonna drive me home see you soon

> > **Me:** 👍

"Hey." I get my parents' attention. "That was Lex. Everything's okay. Jack's bringing her home."

Mom sighs in relief, but Dad still looks concerned. "I think there's one more person I have to talk to," he says.

"Yeah, the pool tech company." Mom rolls her eyes, and I know she's thinking about how much it will cost to fix whatever it was that caused the chlorine tanks to leak.

"No," Dad says. "They can't really help. I was just talking to Jack on the phone. He said this—this large knob here—was turned, and it shouldn't have been. He turned it back so I can't tell, but everything seems to be working fine now. The alarm has reset, and nothing is leaking."

"Then who do you have to talk to?" Mom presses her lips together. My heart races. I know it's not good.

"That police officer in the parking lot," he says. "I think someone turned the knob on purpose."

I suck in my breath. Lucas. It has to be Lucas. He said he didn't know what he would do.

He did this.

Chapter 12

"On purpose?" Mom says.

"I can't say for sure, but Jack says after the alarm sounded, this knob was turned to the left, and he absolutely turned it off. I showed him this stuff when he started lifeguarding." Dad puts his hands on his hips. "And the only way he would turn it off is if someone had turned it on."

"Like the same person who vandalized our pool with ketchup and eggs?" I blurt.

Dad looks at me like he doesn't even remember the vandalism. "Uh, no, hon. And anyway, that's a matter for me and the police to discuss. You don't need to worry about it."

I don't say anything more.

I duck away from my parents and check Lucas's Instagram. The pic I saw this morning was posted at 6:58 a.m., and he posted another pic of him and his teammates having breakfast after practice at 8:41 a.m. He could have gotten here in between those times if someone drove him—someone like his brother.

But the first caption said he was going to practice, and the second caption said *breakfast wi the team*. So, he was probably at practice from seven until eight thirty, and the leak happened at seven thirty. Do these pics mean he didn't do it? Or do they mean he did it, and he's trying to cover it up? My head spins.

Dad heads toward the exit. "I'm going to talk to the police officer for a few minutes. Kim, you can take Maddie home. I might be a little while."

I wonder if I should tell my dad about Lucas, but my throat tightens. I was so sure it was Lucas when the leak first happened, but now, I don't know. He was probably at his own practice all morning, like he said in the pics.

And Dad wants me not to worry about it. And if he thinks I'm worrying about it, then he'll think I'm not managing my anxiety. And I don't want to talk about Lucas anyway.

"I can go home by myself," I squeak. I don't need my parents watching over me like I'm a toddler.

"No, hon," Mom says. "You still look a little shaken. I'll take you home and get you some breakfast. But first, we need to go in the clubhouse and make a sign for the door that we're closed for the rest of the day."

"Okay," I relent. I'd forgotten that I haven't eaten anything yet today. I look at my phone. It's only 8:50. The whole thing didn't take as long as it felt. Ez had jumped in the water at 7:29. I realize that the 11–12s and 9–10s will be arriving for practice soon, so I tell my parents, "I'll post that we're closed so people don't start showing up expecting a workout."

"Good point," Mom says. "I'll make some calls too.

But not too many. I want to get you home and fed." Mom puts her arm around my shoulders and leads me into the clubhouse.

The clubhouse is between the boys' and girls' locker rooms, behind the Snack Shack. You can get to the clubhouse through the locker rooms, but there's also a main entrance that faces the parking lot. My dad fixed the lock on that entrance after the ketchup incident, so no one should have been able to get into the pool area through the clubhouse.

Mom and I enter the clubhouse through the girls' locker room. I glance at the tile that got that tiny crack when Charlotte dropped her shaving cream and hope Mom doesn't get close enough to notice. After everything that's happened today, that might just be the thing that makes her ready to sell the whole club.

We exit the locker room into a hallway near the racquetball courts. The clubhouse also has a yoga room, a weight room, and a decent-sized event room with a small kitchen and office off to the side. It's not much compared to a big gym like FitWest, but it's comfortable, and our loyal members keep us in business over the winter with yoga classes and racquetball and squash groups.

While Mom makes some phone calls, I grab a couple of sheets of paper and some markers from the office to make closed signs. I figure we'll need one for the gate, one for the clubhouse, and a couple for the parking lot.

I think about how Lucas's brother Derek will

probably be happy we have to close again. I channel all my anger toward the Bryce brothers into making the signs pretty with doodles of fish and eels and sunshine.

It might be a little excessive, because when Mom finishes her calls she says over my shoulder, "I think they'll get the message."

"Yeah, I guess." I gather the signs and put the markers away in the office.

"Ready for breakfast?" Mom tries to look enthusiastic, but the circles under her eyes tell me she's stressed and tired.

But I'm still going to let her make me breakfast. "Yep, let's go."

I grab my bag and remember the tiny polar bear that's zipped in the inner pocket. I still can't bring myself to tell my parents about it, with all that's going on and how much they already worry. I saw the look on Mom's face when I was doing my breathing in the parking lot. She's not sure I can handle my anxiety when something serious happens.

The sun beats down as Mom and I walk home, but the thought of that polar bear covers my arms in goose bumps.

Dad comes home while we're eating pancakes and gives us the rundown of his talk with the police. They checked the area and couldn't find anything suspicious, so the leak has been ruled an accident and unrelated to the vandalism since there was no evidence of a break-in.

I think differently, but I don't tell him that. He says that it's actually a good thing it was ruled an accident, because then we're less likely to be liable for any damages or injuries. I didn't even realize we could be liable, and I guess chlorine gas poisoning counts as an injury, even when the person who got it is my best friend.

Later in the afternoon, I get a text from Ez.

Ez: i'm home

Me: can I come over?

Ez: yeah for a little bit

Me: ok see you soon

As soon as I text it, I want to take it back. I don't know if I want to see Ez. I don't know if I want to see her looking weak and tired and sick. But I do want to tell her about my texts with Lucas last night and see what she thinks. I didn't have time to tell her before the chlorine leaked.

I also want to know that she's okay.

When I get to Ez's house, her mom answers the door. I don't see Ez's mom much. She works a lot, and it's just the two of them.

"Hey, Maddie," Ez's mom whispers, and opens the door wider to let me in.

"Oh," I whisper back. "Is Ez sleeping?"

"No, just resting." Ez's mom wrinkles her eyebrows. "I don't really know why I'm whispering," she says a little louder. "Come in, she's in her room."

I walk down the hall and hover at the doorway to Ez's room. She's sitting on her bed, frowning at something on her phone.

"Don't just stand there," Ez says without looking up. "I'm not contagious. But what the heck? Everyone is posting about the pool being closed the whole holiday weekend."

"What?" I hurry to sit next to her on her bed. "No, we're just closed today. Dad says things are fine. Tell them!"

"I will," Ez says. "But seriously? This one guy is saying that he saw cops there all morning and it's now a crime zone. Why would he think that?"

I look away. "Actually, there was a cop who stayed all morning."

"What? Why?"

I tell Ez about Dad talking to the police officer, and how he thinks someone turned the knob on purpose.

"I think it was Lucas," I say quietly.

"I hate that kid!" Ez yells. Then she coughs a few times. Yelling is probably not the best idea when recovering from gas poisoning.

"Yeah, me too. But my dad doesn't think the leak has anything to do with the vandalism, and definitely not the glass. It's like he doesn't even remember the other stuff that happened." I pick at a thread on Ez's pillow.

"So, what did the police say?" she asks.

"That nothing can be proven. Jack turned the knob off, obviously, so by the time they got there, there wasn't really any evidence that anything had happened at all. They didn't even say 'Just a prank,'" I explain. "They're ruling it an accident."

"An accident? No way." Ez coughs again and takes a sip from her water bottle.

"Actually, it's good for us, for the club. It means we're less likely to be, um, liable." I suddenly remember the incident at River Oaks where the girl's parents sued the club after she was cut. My heart rate picks up.

I think Ez remembers it, too, because she quickly says, "Oh. No. I would never think you were liable for this. This was totally not your parents' fault."

"But it was someone's fault." I look down. "Maybe it was my fault."

Suddenly Ez doesn't look sick at all. "No. If Lucas did this, it was his fault, not yours."

I show Ez last night's conversation with Lucas on my phone. "What about this?"

She reads through the messages. "Okay, that is super creepy. Why would you ask a girl out and then say you don't know what you'll do when she says no? That's a sure way to never get girls to talk to you ever."

"I know." I shudder. "But I think that's why he did it—the leak. To get back at me."

"If he did, that just makes him an even worse person

than we thought. None of this is even close to your fault." Ez smacks the pillow next to her in emphasis.

"I know that logically, but I just feel like I should have done something different, somewhere. Told him I didn't like him sooner or something. Or been nicer to him."

"Maddie, you were nice to him. Nicer than he deserved. What were you supposed to do? Pretend you like him when you don't?" Ez smooths out her pillowcase. "And it doesn't matter anyway, because I don't even think it was him. I mean, wouldn't we have noticed him at practice this morning?"

"Yeah, I thought that too." I pull up Lucas's Instagram. "Look." I show Ez. "He totally could have pulled the chlorine alarm between taking these pictures."

"I don't know." Ez looks at the picture. "In this pic, he's obviously at his pool at seven, so even if someone, like his brother, drove him straight from there to our practice, he would have gotten to our pool at like seven fifteen? Seven twenty? I totally would have noticed him. I got to practice at seven twenty."

Ez is making sense. Maybe it wasn't Lucas at all. And if it's not Lucas, I won't have to tell my parents about him and make them think I'm not handling my anxiety. I like thinking that the person responsible might not be Lucas—that maybe this whole thing has nothing to do with me.

But it doesn't help us figure out who did it. "Yeah. I guess," I say. "I don't think we should rule him out yet, but I do think we should get more information before telling my parents about him."

Before Ez can respond, her mom appears in the doorway. "Everything okay in here? You got loud."

"Yeah, Mom, all good." Ez gives her mom a thumbs-up.

"Okay, hon. Five more minutes, then Maddie has to go so you can rest."

Ez flops back onto the pillow. "I can't believe this is happening. I can't believe someone is sabotaging the pool, and worse, that I have to miss two days of practice."

"Only two days? Like, today and tomorrow? So that means you're okay, right?"

"Yeah, yeah, I'm okay." Ez forces a smile. "The doctors gave me some stuff and said I might have more coughing and some nausea, and I'll be tired, but I can get in the water again Friday if I feel okay. Not a full workout, but I can work up to it."

"Good." I'm relieved Ez won't be out of practice for long.

"Hey." Ez grins. "If it's not Lucas, maybe this just means that I'm, like, so good that the teams we swim against are afraid of me."

"So, you think you're the target? Huh. That's bold." I laugh. I do love Ez's confidence.

"Yep. And somewhere out there is an evil plot to take over the swim league." Ez's voice gets lower. "Seriously though, I bet whoever it is, it's someone who's been to the pool, someone we've seen before."

"This weekend will be packed for the holiday," I say. "We'll watch everyone. Anyone doing anything suspicious, we'll have to investigate, ask questions, follow them around, anything."

"Exactly." Ez smiles. Then she sighs, and her face looks slightly gray again.

I stand up and move to the door. "I should go. All this talking is wearing you out."

"I'm okay," she says. "But my mom thinks I should rest."

"So, text me later?"

"You got it."

I feel a little better as I leave Ez's house. I don't like seeing her tired, but I do like seeing her interested in taking down whoever it is who's sabotaging our team. Knowing Ez, she'll be back winning races before the East Valley Vandal can strike again.

All that talking wore me out, too, so as soon as I get home, I crawl into bed and sleep.

When I wake up, shadows cross my window and I know it's almost dinnertime. I reach for my phone. There's a message from Nico.

Nico: heard the pools closed

that sucks

do you still want to hang out tonight

> like somewhere else?

The message is over an hour old. I do want to hang out with Nico. But I can't. I don't know why, but I just can't get up and get dressed and be cute and flirty.

> Me: cant have to do family stuff

He writes back right away.

> Nico: tomorrow?

> Me: ok hopefully pool will be open

> Nico: cool see you then

I think the pool will be open tomorrow. I think the pool will need to be open to make up for missing today and probably tomorrow morning. But I don't know.

I scroll through my Instagram and my group chats. Everyone on the team is talking about what happened this morning. Charlotte even made a TikTok to some old song called "Take My Breath Away." I kind of think it's too soon, but it's a little funny. And she's already got a couple hundred likes on it. Charlotte's a great swimmer, but she might be an even better TikTok-er.

Then there's a post from Derek Bryce, acting all concerned. He reposted that same empty pic of the pool from earlier and wrote *Prayers are with East Valley today. Glad everyone is okay.* It's so gross that he acts like he cares.

It makes me wonder again if he's the one behind this. Would Derek have put his brother up to it? Or just used his brother's past as inspiration? Could a guy as big as Derek have snuck into the pool this morning, opened the gate on the tanks, turned a knob, and left without anyone seeing him?

I know the clubhouse wasn't broken into, but Derek could have arrived super early and hidden in the bushes or something. No one really pays attention to the area behind the tanks with all the brambles. I guess it's possible. Maybe Lucas even told him how to do it, then posted the pics so we wouldn't suspect him.

Disrupting my thoughts, Mom hollers up at me that a pizza's here, and I realize that I'm starving. It really is dinnertime.

Before bed, I scroll through both Lucas's and Derek's Instagrams again to try to find some answers, but nothing makes sense. I pull out my sketchbook and hope it will settle my thoughts.

I map out the pool deck like a blueprint. Maybe if I draw the scene of the crime, I'll figure out how it happened.

I try to keep my drawing to scale, sketching the chlorine tanks the right distance from the locker room. I draw the little three-sided wooden fence around the tanks and pencil in the blackberry bushes and chainlink fence that make up that fourth side.

Studying the sketch, everything looks right. Pool, tanks, bushes, locker room. I have the right layout, but nothing is telling me how someone could have gotten to the tanks without anyone noticing.

Frustrated, I throw the sketchbook back in my drawer and dive under my covers.

Chapter 13

Thursday morning, the sun doesn't come up. Practice has been canceled for the fire department check, so I haven't set an alarm, and I sleep until nearly eleven a.m. I could have slept longer, but I hear the door slam and figure there might be news. Outside my bedroom window, dull gray clouds cover the sky.

"Good news, Mad!" Dad hollers when I make it down to the kitchen. He's definitely excited because my ears ring when he talks. "The fire department cleared the pool of all danger! We can open this afternoon! I've got the Snack Shack deliveries coming at three, so we open at four o'clock! Get on the socials!"

"Okay, Dad, just—I mean, it looks like it's gonna rain." I yawn and reach for the cereal.

"Nope, no rain in the forecast. It's summer. It doesn't rain in the summer here." Dad looks his phone. "Okay, well, maybe a little rain is in the forecast but not until late tonight, and as long as there's no thunder, which is highly unlikely, we can swim."

"All right, I'll spread the word." He's right—we don't get much rain in the summer here, but one or two days early on we'll get a shower. It always takes us by surprise.

I post a few notices on my social medias, and text the team group chat that the pool will be open tonight. I text Nico, too, but our hangout is feeling less and less exciting.

There's something about overcast weather that makes me want to paint, so in the afternoon, before I have to deal with the busy pool and the people, I put on leggings and a sweater and head outside to my easel. I like painting outside in natural light, so my parents let me keep it on the patio under the awning.

I open my tubes of paint and start mixing blues and greens. I don't realize it at first—I think I'm just painting leaves and branches—but after a few brushstrokes I realize I'm painting blackberry bushes against a clear blue sky. I mix up some purple to go with the bushes. The painting flows better than the sketch I tried to draw last night.

I don't know how much time passes, but when my fingers cramp and my legs get sore from standing, I step back and examine my work.

It's an okay painting, I guess—it's just a bunch of bushes—but the colors contrast nicely, and the leaves look real. I even remembered to put in the thorns. Painting didn't help me figure out anything about who's sabotaging our pool, but it did help me feel better. And it's much less anxiety-producing than scanning the Bryce brothers' Instagram accounts for clues. I clean up my paints and head to the pool.

Dad's earlier energy is not exactly matched that

evening. When I get to the pool at five, Dad is fussing in the Snack Shack, Lexi is sitting on the lifeguard chair, and Jack is in the shallow end tossing a water polo ball with a bunch of 15–18s.

I spread my blanket in the usual spot and slide up to Lexi. "I thought Jack was supposed to be working?"

"He was." Lexi sighs. "But he got bored. I mean, look around."

I do, and I see what she means. The only people at the pool are kids my age and older, mostly from swim team. It seems like a lot of people because sixteen-year-old boys are *really* loud, but it's not.

"Something's missing," I say.

"Yeah. Kids." Lexi's right. Usually there are families around. Babies crawling on blankets and 6-and-unders playing in the shallow end. But no one here is under thirteen.

"Is it the weather?" I wonder. It hasn't rained yet, but dark clouds hang in the sky. "It's warm, but it's gloomy."

"I don't think it's the weather." Lexi sighs. "I think it's that we had a major accident here yesterday, and no one wants to bring their little kids."

My heart sinks. "I was hoping it wasn't that."

For a second, I wonder if I should tell Lexi about Lucas and how I suspect he's behind the vandalism. But she would tell my parents and Jack, and everyone would be on my case about how I can't handle stressful situations.

"It'll be okay." Lexi smiles. She's doing that

act-positive-around-Maddie thing again, but I know she's not really sure that it'll be okay. Guess I won't be telling her about Lucas after all.

I help Dad sort and prep snacks for a while. We manage to do a decent burger business with all the teenagers. Around seven, I see my friends. Sophie and Jess come in holding hands, and not long after, Aidan, Owen, and Nico walk through the gate.

My heart skips when I see Nico. Aidan and Owen plop right onto my blanket on the grass as though I laid it out just for them, but Nico stands and surveys the pool deck. I think he's looking for me.

I hope he's looking for me.

I let him wonder for another few seconds before I step out from behind the Snack Shack and wave. He was definitely looking for me, because his face breaks out into a huge grin and he waves back before sitting next to his cousin. It's pretty cute, and I'm pretty sure I have a huge grin to match.

"Hey, Dad, I'm gonna take a break," I tell him as he cleans some trays from the freezer.

"Sure. Take a pretzel or two," he says. I'm not even sure Dad really needed me in the Shack. I think he just knew I needed something to do before my friends showed up.

I pull two big soft pretzels out of the warmer and take them over to my friends.

"Maaadddiiee!!" Owen yells. "I hope you're bringing those for us." I set one tray right in front of him and

Aidan and hand the other one to Jess, who's sitting on the blanket with her back against Sophie's legs.

"You're lucky you're in good with the owner," I say to Owen, then smile at Nico, who is not paying any attention to the pretzels but is definitely paying attention to me.

My stomach quivers. "Hi," I say, sitting between him and Aidan.

"Hi," he says back. Aidan pulls off half a pretzel and makes a moan-y noise that is either showing great appreciation for the deliciousness that is pretzel or making fun of his cousin. Either way, I blush.

"Hey, where's Charlotte?" I ask.

"Out of town," Sophie offers. "She posted a TikTok earlier from Bodega Bay."

"Sounds nice," I say.

Sophie shrugs. "Eh, I'd rather be hanging out with my friends than off isolated with my family."

"Got that right." Jess grabs Sophie's hand.

"It was a good TikTok though," Owen mumbles through pretzel. "Like, it was all beach in the sunset and very dramatic."

"She does love being dramatic." I roll my eyes.

Aidan and Owen continue making unintelligible noises and eating the pretzel. I should have brought three. Or ten.

"Maddie, you make the best pretzels." Aidan squeezes my knee in praise while using his other hand to stuff pretzel in his face. "I'm so happy I get to be in your friend zone."

"Um, thanks, A, but I just took them out of the warmer and put salt on them." I laugh.

"But you did it very, very well." Owen sits up. "Hey, do we have to wait an hour before swimming, since the pretzel is not a full meal?"

"Do you even wait an hour after eating before eating again?" Jess snarks.

"Good point!" Owen stands up and takes off his shirt.

"Hey, Mad," Jess says. "How's Ez?"

I get a little quiet. Ez had texted me earlier that she couldn't hang out tonight, and she really wants to come to practice tomorrow. She won't be able to do a full workout yet, but she wants to try a few laps.

"She's okay," I tell everyone. "Just tired. She should be here in the morning."

"Good," Sophie says. "God, that was terrifying yesterday."

"I know." I pick at the grass.

"Yeah," Aidan says. "You're lucky you're not a swimmer, coz." He pats Nico on the arm, then leans his head on my shoulder.

"Was everyone else okay?" Nico asks.

"Yeah," I say. "Ez got the worst of it."

"Do they know what happened?" Sophie asks. "I mean, how it happened?"

I don't know if I should tell everyone that someone

did it on purpose, and I definitely don't want to talk about my suspicions about Lucas or Derek Bryce.

"Police ruled it an accident." I leave it at that.

"Seems like a lot of accidents around here this summer," Sophie says as she eats the last of a pretzel. I don't think she's trying to be rude, but I don't know how to respond to that, and I don't want to talk about accidents anymore, so I clean up the pretzel plates and napkins.

"I better go see if my dad needs help," I say as I head back to the Snack Shack.

About a half an hour later, Nico edges up to the Snack Shack. The rest of the group is in the water now, playing with the water polo ball from Jack and his friends.

I step outside the Shack. "Hey," I say, looking up at Nico's dark-brown eyes. He's nearly a head taller than me.

"You okay?" he asks. "You seemed a little, I don't know, upset?"

It's sweet that he notices. And sweet that he doesn't make me feel weird about it. "I'm okay, it's just weird to be here without Ez. And weird that just yesterday we were in the middle of an emergency. It's just . . ."

"Weird?" He smiles.

"Yeah."

"That makes sense." Nico takes his hands in and out of his pockets. "So, I have to go, but will you, um, will you walk out with me?"

I glance back at my dad working the grill. He must have heard, because he waves me off. Dad might not think I can handle my anxiety, but at least he believes I can handle a boy.

"Sure," I say. We walk down the pool deck to the gate.

When we get out of the gate and into the parking lot, Nico takes my hand and laces his fingers through mine. A shiver runs up my arm. No one else is in the parking lot, and when he stops walking and faces me, I suddenly wonder if he's going to kiss me. I've never kissed anyone before, but I want to, and I'm pretty sure I want it to be this boy.

But he doesn't kiss me. He just stops and looks at me for a second. My stomach quivers again. He has really pretty eyes.

Nico takes my other hand and brings it to his face. "Looks like we've both been doing a little painting?" He touches a spot of blue paint on my hand that didn't get washed off.

The gesture makes my face hot. "Yeah, but mine was on an easel, not a wall."

He lights up. "You paint? Like an artist?"

I nod. "Well, I don't know if I'm an artist, but I, like, do art stuff."

"Cool. Maybe I could see your work sometime?" His eyes sparkle.

I can't concentrate on whether or not I want him to see my paintings and drawings because I'm too busy thinking about how his hand feels on mine, so I mutter, "Yeah, maybe."

"But not this weekend." He sighs. "I have to go away

for the holiday. I'm really bummed I can't just be at the pool all weekend and hang out with you and everyone."

"That's okay," I say. I'm disappointed that he won't be around, but the way he said it was so cute that I can't really be too upset. "Where are you going?"

"Colorado. My dad lives there."

"Okay. So, text me?"

He beams. "Definitely." He lets go of my hand to give me a big hug. He smells good, like some kind of citrus-fruit shampoo and a little bit of paint, and not at all like chlorine, which is nice for a change.

When he loosens his hug, he takes my hand again and starts walking away. He doesn't drop my hand until he absolutely has to. "Bye, Maddie."

"Bye, Nico." I watch him walk down the street. I don't want to go back to the pool until I can't see him anymore. Before he gets to the corner, he turns and waves at me, sending the flutters flying in my stomach again.

I head back into the pool, trying to hide my grin. I'm sure I'm blushing again. I think about how he looked at me right before I thought he might kiss me. I'm pretty sure he was thinking about it too.

After the pool closes, my dad goes into the clubhouse to get the receipts in order, and Lexi, Jack, and I are left with the outdoor cleanup. Clouds hover in the sky, and I pull my sweatshirt on. I realize I haven't thought about

Lucas all evening because I've been too busy thinking about Nico, and I smile to myself.

Jack is wiping down chairs when he hollers across the pool, "Hey, Lex! Does Maddie have a boyfriend?"

Lexi's picking up loose trash and hollers back, "I don't know, dude. Ask her yourself."

"Hey, Maddie! Do you have a boyfriend?" Jack yells at me.

I pick up some trash and walk it over to the garbage can. "None of your business." I roll my eyes dramatically. I'm not embarrassed, or even really annoyed. Jack teasing me about boys is Jack's way of showing brotherly affection.

"I like him," Jack says.

"No one asked you." I throw a wadded-up napkin at him.

"No, really! He's not like most guys, who like to show off how good they are at stuff." Jack puffs up his chest. "I mean, I personally *am* good at stuff, so it's not like I'm showing off. But your guy, he just kind of chills."

I smile. "I didn't know you were paying so much attention."

"Hey, I care about who's chilling around my little sister."

Lexi joins us at the garbage can. "Maybe when you're lifeguarding you should care a little more about what's happening in the pool than out of it?"

"Hey, I am a fantastic lifeguard. Here, I'll show you."

Jack makes a move like he's going to push Lexi in the pool.

Lexi pushes him back. "Don't even think about it. I have a date in like five minutes. Kari's on her way."

"What? A date? Why are my sisters getting all the good action around here? What am I? Fish food?" Jack wipes a fake tear from his face.

I give him a little push. "Please, you know the girls all adore you. If only they knew you've given your heart to pizza."

"Mmmm. I love pizza. Let's order some after our dear sister leaves for her date."

Lexi picks up a towel that someone left behind. "That dark-haired boy is pretty cute though, Mad."

"I know." I grin. "Hey, speaking of cute . . ." I point to the pool gate, where a girl with pink hair wearing a T-shirt and a denim skirt walks in.

"Kari!" Jack yells, and runs over to her, looping his arm through hers and escorting her over to Lexi. He leans his head next to Kari's. "So, where are we going on our date? How do you feel about pizza?"

Lexi laughs. "Hey! That's *my* date. And we're going for sushi. You have a date with pizza. Only pizza. Just you and one big pizza all night long."

Jack sighs. "That really is my favorite date. No complications."

"Hi, Maddie," Kari says. "Got stuck cleaning up with these two again?"

"Yep, family business, you know how it goes."

"Can I steal her yet?" Kari asks, linking her hand with Lexi's.

"Sure, we're almost done," I say. "Jack and I will finish up."

"Hey!" Jack says. "Speak for yourself. I have a date with a pizza. Your date already left."

"You had a date?" Kari lifts her eyebrows at me.

Lexi smiles. "Maddie was spotted chatting with a cute dark-haired new boy."

"Ooh, new is always good." Kari smiles.

Now I'm getting red. Just as everyone is looking at me, a raindrop splashes on my face.

"Is it raining?" I frown.

"Happens once a summer." Jack shakes a fist at the sky. "Darn global warming."

As the rain falls a little harder, Lexi pulls Kari toward the exit. "Let's get out of here. I've had enough water today!" They wave and hurry out the gate.

Jack puts an arm around my shoulder. "Fine. C'mon, Mad, let's go see if Dad will buy me—I mean, us—a pizza."

I duck my head as we hurry toward the clubhouse. "This rain sucks. 'Specially with the holiday coming."

"It's always a bad time for rain when your business is in recreational swimming," Jack says. "But it's better than a chlorine leak."

Chapter 14

It doesn't feel like anything could be worse than rainy weather on Fourth of July weekend. The rain stopped in time for us to have practice on Friday morning, but it was cold and miserable, and everyone couldn't wait to get out.

Saturday afternoon, Ez and I are at the pool, curled up on chaise lounges and not about to get in the water. I'm wearing my suit under my sweats, but I don't even know why I put it on. It's not raining anymore; it's just cloudy and cool. I'm not the only one who thinks so, because for a Saturday on a holiday weekend, the pool is pretty empty.

Our friends aren't even around. Since it's one of the few summer weekends with no swim meet, most of the team takes the opportunity to get out of town. Sophie, Jess, and Aidan are all camping with their families in various parts of the state, Nico is still at his dad's, Owen's family went to San Francisco for the weekend, and Charlotte is still in Bodega Bay.

"This sucks." I sigh.

"At least I got a little practice in yesterday," Ez says.

"Yeah, you feel better?" I lean forward in my chaise lounge.

Ez pulls her navy-blue beanie down over her ears and frowns. "I do feel better. I feel like all my muscles are working, and I know I can do everything I've ever done. But I'm tired. I just feel like I don't have the energy for what I need to do."

I've never seen Ez like this. Defeated. I hate it.

"You'll get it back," I tell her. "At least there's no meet this week. By next week, I know you'll get it back."

"I hope so." Ez picks at the peeling plastic on the chaise lounge—one more thing that needs replacing around here. "You know, they told me that fatigue could be a symptom of alopecia, because it's an autoimmune thing. But I've never had it before."

"You've also never had chlorine poisoning before. I'm sure it will be better soon." I muster all my positive energy. "You know what would help? Soft pretzels."

Ez smiles. "Yes, absolutely. Pretzel me, please."

"Be right back." I walk over to the Snack Shack, where my dad looks busy cleaning and organizing. He can't actually be busy though, since no one is here to order snacks.

I lean over the counter. "Hey, Dad. Can we get some pretzels?"

He looks up as though I've interrupted an important thought. "Oh, hi, hon. Yeah, pretzels. Okay. Only, I just turned off the warmer since no one was ordering. Give me a few minutes to warm it up."

"Okay, thanks." It's not like I'm in a hurry anyway.

"You don't have to wait. Go be with your friends." I don't think he realizes that Ez is my only friend here today. "I'll bring them out to you when they're ready."

When Dad comes over a few minutes later with two giant salty pretzels, he sits on the empty chaise lounge next to Ez and hands her a pretzel.

"So, Esmeralda," he says. "It's good to see you here. How are you feeling?"

Ez shrugs. "Okay. A little tired."

A worried look crosses Dad's face. "I'm so sorry this happened here, at our pool. We've been wanting to update the chlorination system, but it's been a busy summer."

"It's okay. I mean, at least I was all dramatic and made everyone get out of here so no one else got hurt." Ez pulls off a chunk of pretzel.

Dad leans forward. "So, is there anything else you remember about that morning? Like, did you see anyone suspicious? I already asked Maddie about this stuff, but I wanted to ask you too."

Interesting. Maybe Dad hasn't let it go like I thought he had.

"Nope," she says.

"What about anyone from the team? Anyone acting funny?" Dad asks.

"What?" I startle. "You think someone from the team caused the leak?" I've been so busy thinking Lucas was our vandal, it didn't even occur to me that it could be someone closer—someone we wouldn't have noticed because we see them all the time.

"No, of course not." Dad shakes his head and stares at the tanks. Then he jumps up, like he suddenly remembered something. "I shouldn't worry you about this. It was just an accident. Enjoy your pretzels!"

I sigh as Dad walks back to the Snack Shack. "He keeps doing that. Talking about all the stuff that's happened and then suddenly deciding he shouldn't be talking about it. That's why I haven't told him about Lucas. It's like he thinks I'm going to combust if even a hint of anxiety comes near me."

"And that might be almost as exciting as a chlorine leak!" Ez laughs. "Okay, no, seriously, you're not going to combust, right?"

"No," I say. "Talking about what's been happening around here and trying to find the vandal actually makes me feel less anxious about it."

Ez nods. "Yep, me too. Let's figure it out so people will come swim here again."

"I still think it was Lucas. I know we don't have any proof, but I just can't see anyone else being so hostile and, like, childish."

"I say we keep an open mind." Ez circles her eyes with her fingers and thumb like a pair of binoculars. "Search for clues and consider all possibilities."

"Nancy Drew back in action?" I hold up my fist.

Ez gives me a fist bump. "We are back on the case of the East Valley Vandal!"

12

By Monday, the official holiday, things are looking much brighter. The sun shines high like it's supposed to on the Fourth of July, and both Jack and Lexi are working. Dad even calls in another lifeguard to handle the crowds.

Holiday crowds are different from regular summer crowds. The pool is packed with visiting out-of-towners. It's a lot of folks I don't recognize. Ez is the only friend I've seen all weekend.

Which is fine because by the afternoon, Dad needs all the help he can get in the Snack Shack. I'm busy scooping cheese on nachos and loading trays with hot dogs, chips, soft pretzels, and Popsicle after Popsicle. Dad always gives free red-white-and-blue Popsicles to kids on the Fourth of July. Last night, I heard Mom arguing that this year he should charge for them, and he was having none of that.

"If kids can't get free red-white-and-blue pops on the Fourth of July, then we've lost all the joy in owning a pool, and we might as well shut down for good!" Dad isn't a yeller, but he has very strong opinions about free Popsicles.

"Well, that just might be an option!" Mom had snapped back.

Ultimately, Dad won out, and today the coolers are full of plastic-wrapped frozen joy.

Around five o'clock, things start to slow down. Ez swings by the Snack Shack, and Dad tells me to take a break. I grab Popsicles, and Ez and I plop down on the grass to watch the crowds.

"Looks like people weren't afraid to come to the pool after all," Ez says.

"Yeah, but they aren't the regulars." I unwrap my Popsicle. "These people probably don't even know that there was a chlorine leak here five days ago."

"Let's not tell them," Ez whispers.

"Agreed." As I'm watching the crowd, I spot a guy sitting all by himself in a folding chair under a tree at the far end of the grass. He's wearing light-blue swim shorts and dark sunglasses.

I suddenly recognize him. "Ez!" I grab her arm and whisper-yell, "That's Lucas's brother! Derek the FitWest guy!" This is the first time I've seen him in person.

Ez leans in to get a closer look. "That guy under the tree? You don't have to whisper. He definitely cannot hear us."

"Oh yeah, probably not. But don't stare," I whisper anyway.

"I saw him when I came in," Ez says. "I thought there was something weird about him. Like, who goes to a crowded pool all by themselves on the Fourth of July?"

As we're staring, Derek is joined by the last person I want to see: Lucas. He sits on the ground next to his brother's chair, a flop of bleached hair in his eyes.

"No! What is Lucas doing here?" I whisper-yell.

"Suspicious!" Ez says. "Why are they at our pool and not River Oaks?"

"They're up to something." I try to keep my stomach from turning over. "Think we can watch them without them seeing us?"

"Maybe if we walk around a little." Ez pulls her straw hat lower on her forehead. "Operation Spy-on-Suspects in progress."

We head around the pool the opposite way from Derek and Lucas's setup. But apparently, we are not very sneaky. As we throw away our Popsicle sticks, Lucas appears next to the garbage can.

"Hey," he says, pushing the hair out of his eyes. "Where'd you get the Popsicles?"

My throat clams up. Ez looks at me, waiting for me to say something. I flash back to the morning of the chlorine leak—how angry I was, and how sure I was that Lucas was the one who caused it.

I find my voice. "Really? You're coming here looking for freebies after what you did? You really want a free Popsicle in exchange for setting off the chlorine alarm and nearly killing my best friend? You don't get any Popsicles. They're not free for you."

"Um, I don't know if I nearly died, exactly," Ez mumbles.

Lucas looks at me like I have Popsicles coming out of my nose. "I haven't set off a chlorine alarm in two years. I don't know what you're talking about."

My heart pounds in my ears. I'm so certain he was the one who sabotaged our pool. "You set it off here. I know you did. You did it because I—"

"You think I would come here and risk getting kicked off another swim team because of you? You're not that special, Maddie," Lucas scoffs. "I had my own practice to go to. I can't run over here in the morning, set off an alarm, and then go to practice. Ask anyone. You want my coach's number? He'll tell you I was at practice when your big alarm went off."

My cheeks burn. "But the glass. You broke the snow globe and left glass on our pool. And the polar bear, with the eggs. So, you had to do the other stuff." My voice trails off. I suddenly feel completely ridiculous for accusing Lucas with no proof. I didn't even think to ask his coach or Daniella or someone else on his team whether or not he was at practice the morning of the leak. I could have found someone to ask. I just didn't think of it because I was so sure it was him.

"What glass? That ugly snow globe?" he blurts. "Yeah, giving that to you was a mistake, obviously. But after I dropped it on the sidewalk, on accident, I never saw it again. Someone else must have cleaned it up."

I don't know what to think anymore. I don't trust Lucas, but the way he's talking makes me feel small and silly—like I'm ridiculous for thinking he's responsible for the vandalism at our pool. A lump forms in my throat.

"Does your dad know who I am?" Lucas demands, face flushed and sweaty.

I shake my head. If I talk, I might start crying, and then I would really feel ridiculous.

"Good." He sneers. "Then I'm getting a free Popsicle."

As Lucas storms off to the Snack Shack, Ez leans over. "I think you're worth getting kicked off a swim team for."

A couple of tears fall down my cheeks, and I wipe them away. "That actually means a lot coming from you."

She squares off and looks me in the eyes. "You okay?"

I swallow the lump in my throat and take a deep breath. "I guess. I hate talking to Lucas. He always makes me feel like I did something wrong."

"That's because he's a liar and a total manipulator. You didn't do anything wrong."

"Do you think he was telling the truth?" I sniffle. "That he didn't do it?"

"I don't trust him at all," Ez says. "Now, let's spy on his brother. I want info."

"You got it." I force a smile for Ez's efforts. "Where'd his brother go?"

"I don't know, but *your* brother is staring at us." Ez points at the lifeguard stand. Jack points at me and gives me a thumbs-up with a shrug, like he's asking if everything's okay.

I give him a thumbs-up in return and nod. I appreciate that Jack is watching out for me, but I don't want him asking a bunch of questions about Lucas later.

We scan the area for signs of Derek. But all we see is Lucas, across the pool. He's found a Popsicle and is currently dripping blue sugar liquid all down his arm.

"Ugh, he did actually get a free Popsicle," I groan. "Jerk."

Ez snorts. "Yeah, but he eats it like a baby, and it's going to permanently stain those ugly shorts he's wearing. So hey, joke's on him. Oh! There's Derek." Ez points across the pool. "Over by the Snack Shack."

"Oh my god, he's about to talk to my dad. C'mon, let's go eavesdrop." I pull her toward the clubhouse. "We should be able to hear everything from the girls' locker room."

In the locker room, it's cool and quiet, and we sit as close as we can to the wall the locker room shares with the Snack Shack. A convenient vent at the top of the wall means we can hear everything.

Dad is super chatty. We hear him say, "You can never predict how a summer business is going to do, you know. But a few things happened that we weren't counting on, like an incident of vandalism."

A deep male voice that I'm assuming is Derek's replies, "I can imagine this would be a hard season. I heard about the chlorine leak. I'm so sorry."

I whisper to Ez, "Yeah, real sorry, I bet."

"Shh!" she puts a finger to her lips.

Dad responds, "Yep, that leak happening before the holiday was bad timing. Uh, I mean, a leak is never good timing, but——"

"Tough break, man, tough break," Derek says. I can't help but roll my eyes at his fake sincerity. And I know it's fake because the next thing he says is, "Have you given any more thought to our offer?"

My heart leaps when Dad says, "I don't think we'll be selling this pool. It's been a hard summer, but it'll come around."

"What if I tell you I can increase that offer by fifteen percent?" Derek says. My heart sinks back down into my feet.

Dad mumbles something that sounds like, "I don't know," or maybe, "You can go." I'm not sure.

Derek replies with, "You have my number, just let me know if there's anything I can help you with. I'll be in touch."

I hurry to the door of the locker room and see both Lucas and Derek walking back to their chair under the tree. Derek folds the chair and packs up his things.

Ez comes up behind me. "He sure picked a convenient time to increase his offer. Right after a bad leak and a disappointing holiday weekend."

"Yeah," I grumble. "I don't think his timing was an accident."

"And the chlorine leak wasn't an accident either," Ez says. "Derek sure knows how to make use of a bad situation."

"Maybe," I say. "Or maybe he knows how to create a bad situation—with the help of his hashtag-little-bro."

Before Ez and I leave the locker room, I glance into the shower where Charlotte was shaving a few weeks ago. The crack in the tile where she dropped her shaving cream bottle has spread. It's now about twice as long as it was. My heart pounds.

Cracks that spread become chips, and the last thing we need is one more chip in the tile.

Chapter 15

Tuesday morning should be practice as usual. But it's not. Charlotte and a few other kids are missing. Lexi tells me that Charlotte had texted her saying they were still on vacation, but she hasn't heard from the others.

Right at the end of practice, my mom shows up. Mom never comes to practice. She sleeps late and handles business matters from home, unless there's an event to prepare or a yoga class to teach, which there isn't right now.

Mom talks to Lexi for a few minutes while our age groups get out and the younger kids get in the water. I don't head to the locker room though; I just take off my cap and walk over to Mom and Lexi.

"What's wrong?" I ask, water dripping off my elbows.

Mom sighs. "Oh nothing, hon. It's fine."

A knob of anger lodges in my throat. I know it's not nothing, and I'm more than a little tired of being left out of family discussions about the pool.

"Not true," I say. "You're never here this early. What's going on?" I wonder if she saw the crack in the shower tile, but I don't think cracked tile would be enough to get Mom here this early.

Lexi turns to me. "You're going to find out eventually anyway. Five of the team's families have left the Eels. They got freaked out about the chlorine leak and don't feel safe here."

The anger in my throat sinks into a puddle of dread in my stomach. That can't be good for business. Or for team spirit.

Mom continues, "I came here because I needed their files from the clubhouse, and to tell Lex they wouldn't be at practice."

"That just sucks." I'm not angry at my mom anymore, but anger still bubbles under my skin. I can't believe people have no loyalty. "It was an accident though. I mean, don't they care about the team?"

Mom shrugs. "Well, they think their kids are in danger. One of them had even threatened to leave the day we found the vandalism."

Lexi picks up a stack of kickboards. "Well, I'm going to get practice going for these kids. You can drop my pay if you have to, Mom."

"That's sweet, honey, but—"

"What does she mean by that?" I interrupt. "Don't you already pay her less than you would someone outside the family?"

Mom inhales deeply. "It's just that the families want their team fees back."

"Well, don't give them back." My skin itches.

"If I don't give them back, they could make things difficult for us." Moms sighs again. "Maybe even involve lawyers. It's better to just let them go and keep things friendly."

"I don't feel very friendly right now," I say.

I don't know why, but that makes Mom smile. "Thanks, hon. I'm going to go finish up the paperwork. See you at home."

When I get my stuff and head out the gate, Ez is waiting for me. "What was that all about?"

I tell her about the families leaving, and she gets angry too. "Ugh! Why are people like that? I'm sorry, Maddie. I know that's hard on you guys."

"It'll be okay," I say. I don't know if I believe that, but it feels like I should say it.

Ez shifts her swim bag to her other shoulder. "So, was Charlotte one of the families?"

"I don't think so. I think she's just out of town still. Why?"

"I got an email last night from the person in charge of the Tomlin training team," Ez says to the ground. "It said the scholarship people will be at our meet this weekend. I'm sure Charlotte got the same one since she's also an applicant."

"Oh. Are you nervous?" My heart rate picks up just thinking about how Ez must be feeling. She seems okay, but she's still recovering from inhaling poisonous gas. I'm not sure she's ready to impress the Tomlin scouts.

"Eh, kind of. But the thing is, if Charlotte knew the

scholarship people are coming this weekend, she'd be at practice. Her parents would have, like, left the family vacation so she could get training in, I'm sure of it. So why isn't she here?"

Saturday morning, we pick up Ez to bring her to the meet. As she and I walk onto the Maple Grove pool deck, I can't help but comment, "Maple Grove, the original puller of the chlorine-leak-alarm. Could they have also triggered ours?"

"I don't know. Maybe," Ez says, dropping her stuff under the 13–14 pop-up.

"We should keep an eye out," I say. "See if we hear anything, you know, like we did at the River Oaks meet. At least this time, we know we won't run into Lucas. He's banned from this pool." I shudder just thinking about him.

Ez organizes her goggles, sunscreen, and snacks. "You keep an eye out. I'd help, but I've got a scholarship to win."

I suddenly feel guilty for forgetting about the scholarship. "Oh yeah! You'll be great. No way Charlotte will do better than you with all the practices she missed."

Ez grimaces. "I don't know. I still feel like I don't have all my energy back."

"You'll get there. I know you will. But I have to go help Mom and Dad set up. I'll come get you for warm-ups."

"Thanks, Mad," Ez says as she lies on a sleeping bag

and pulls her hat over her face. As much as I believe in Ez's swimming abilities, I'm worried about her. She hasn't smiled much this morning, and swim meets are her favorite thing.

I step out of the pop-up and go to the scoring table to gather the event list and Sharpies to write our event numbers on our arms and the arms of the littler kids.

As I'm heading back to the tent, Owen and Aidan bound over to me. "Mad! What am I swimming?" Aidan gives me a bear hug while Owen snatches the list.

"Oooh, we are gonna kill it in the medley relay. Great lineup," Owen says.

I return Aidan's hug, then push him off. "That's a lot of hugging, A. What's the occasion?"

He walks with me back to the team pop-ups. "I just missed you."

"Dude, I saw you yesterday at practice." I nudge his arm.

"Oh, right," he says with a skip. "It's actually my cousin who misses you. He's coming later."

My face warms when I think of seeing Nico. "So, he's back from Colorado."

"Oh look, you're blushing!" Owen grins. "He's back. Just got back yesterday, and the first thing he wants to do is come to a swim meet and see cute Maddie."

That only makes me blush more. But then I see something that makes all the warmth drain from my face.

It's Charlotte. But she's not under our team pop-up. And she's not wearing our Eels' blue-and-yellow colors.

She's wearing a dark-green Maple Grove suit under her sweatpants, and she's standing among the Maple Grove team tents.

"*Oh.*" I stop in my tracks.

"What?" Aidan looks up. "*Oh.*"

Owen follows our gazes. "Duuuuuudddee."

Then Charlotte sees us. Her face drops into a frown, and she stops talking to the Maple Grove girl next to her.

Owen, Aidan, and I just stand there, in the middle of the field of pop-up tents, staring at her and not moving.

Charlotte lowers her eyes and comes over to us. "Hi," she says.

I open and close my mouth a few times. "Uh, hi?" I manage.

Aidan gives her a hug like he just gave me a hug. "Char! Good to see you! But, uh, dude? What the heck is this green suit you're wearing?"

"Yeah. My parents kind of made me." Charlotte doesn't make eye contact.

Owen narrows his eyes. "Made you betray your teammates and swim for our biggest rivals?"

Aidan whispers, "These are our biggest rivals? I didn't know we had a biggest rival."

"Dude, shh," Owen mutters.

I'm not really listening to the boys. I can't believe Charlotte switched teams. I look at our medley relay list, and her name is down to swim fly on Medley A. That means Lexi didn't even know she'd switched teams.

"I guess we missed a TikTok or two where you decided

CATHERINE ARGUELLES

to tell people you don't swim for our team anymore?"
There's ice in my voice.

"I'm sorry, Maddie." Charlotte's eyes shine. "I didn't
want to leave. I just, my parents—after the chlorine
leak, they said they can't count on the Eels to give me
good practice. And the Tomlin scholarship people are
here."

The scholarship people. Crap. I have to tell Ez about
Charlotte switching teams. Ez and Charlotte are competitors, but they've always been competitors on the
same team. Their competition helps our team win. Ez
is going to feel betrayed.

"You're still listed on our medley, Charlotte." I hold
up the event list. "You could have at least told my sister.
She's counting on you."

"I know, I know. I just didn't know how." She seems
genuinely sad, but I don't really care about her feelings
right now.

"You couldn't have made a TikTok about it? Gone
live on Instagram? Come up with some high-drama
YouTube video?" I'm seething, but I realize I haven't
seen much social media from Charlotte lately.

Charlotte drops her head and says, "I don't have my
phone right now."

That's a shock, but I don't want her to think I care.
"Whatever. Just don't be asking for your money back."
I turn on my heel and head back to Ez.

I hate to have to tell her bad news. Ez is inside the
sleeping bag with her hat over her face, and she looks

like she's actually asleep. Just as I open my mouth to stammer out the words, Lexi runs up and grabs my arm.

"Maddie!" Lexi's face is red and puffy, and not because she's out of breath—because she's angry. "I need you to swim fly in Medley A. I just found out about Charlotte."

"What?" I say. "I can't swim in Medley A."

"Huh?" Ez pops up in the sleeping bag. I guess she wasn't asleep. "What happened with Charlotte? I thought I was swimming fly."

"Charlotte doesn't swim for us anymore. She swims for Maple Grove now," Lexi blurts. "Ezzie, I want you to anchor in free this time. You have the fastest free time anyway. Maddie, I need you in at fly."

"Wait, go back." Ez throws the sleeping bag off her. "Charlotte? Swims for Maple Grove? As of today?"

"Yeah." I look down. "We just found out. Her parents made her leave after the leak."

Ez looks almost as pale as she did when she inhaled poison gas. "That's brutal."

Lexi sighs. "Look, I have to go organize a few more things, but Maddie, please. Fly is the third leg. Sophie should get us a good lead, so all you and Jess have to do is not get us too far behind. Ez will make up the difference in the anchor."

A hint of a smile returns to Ez's face. "Yeah, you can do it, Mad. It'll be okay."

If my pounding heart is any indication, adrenaline alone should make me swim fast. "Fine. I'll do it," I relent.

But when we get to the blocks, I wish I'd said no. I find out that Charlotte's swimming fly for Maple Grove's Team A. Which means I'm swimming against her. As usual, Charlotte's parents are right by the blocks making sure she's ready. But she doesn't fight them this time; she just focuses on the pool, determination in her eyes.

I'm not the only Eel rattled by Charlotte's departure. The whole race is a mess. Sophie gets off to a bad start in the backstroke, then miscounts her strokes and slams her arm into the wall, which worries Jess enough to get a slow start in the breast. She never recovers, and by the time I take off for the fly leg, we're a full second behind Maple Grove.

I actually do a decent fly, thanks to the adrenaline and eight years of competitive swimming, but it's not enough. Charlotte is on fire off the blocks, and I'd have to do a lot more than just "not get too far behind" in order to keep us in the race.

Any other day, Maple Grove's freestyler would be no match for Ez, but by the time Ez leaves the blocks, she can't make up the time and we have to settle for second.

It's devastating to Ez. Usually the medley is a sure win for Eels' Team A and helps her get pumped for a good meet. When Ez gets out of the water after the relay, she doesn't even wait for me. She just grabs her towel and heads for the pop-up. I think she might be crying.

I know it's not my fault—relays are about the whole team—but I can't help feeling like I let Ez down.

A peal of familiar laughter distracts me from Ez's

sadness. I turn to see Charlotte celebrating with her team, laughing about something I didn't hear. Hot anger fills my belly.

More than ever, I want Ez to get that scholarship. I want Ez to beat Charlotte in every race, and I want the Eels to kick the crap out of Maple Grove in this meet today. I hope Ez is up for it.

Chapter 16

Ez is not up for it. The meet doesn't go well for Ez, and it doesn't go well for the Eels.

I don't know if it's the shock of seeing Charlotte on the other team, or the residual effects of chlorine poisoning, but none of Ez's races go well. She still wins the 50 fly, but she takes third in the IM and second in the 50 free, and her fly time is nowhere near her best. None of her times are anywhere near her best.

When she climbs out of the water after her disappointing 50 free, she searches the crowd instead of coming straight for her towel. She finds a woman I don't recognize who looks about our moms' age. It must be the scholarship recruiter. Ez met her at a Tomlin event for new recruits last spring.

I watch them talk for a minute and then find Ez on the way back to our pop-up, where she throws herself into a fold-up chair and puts her head in her hands.

"Hey." I want to tell her "Good race" or something encouraging like that, but it wasn't a good race for her, and Ez hates fake praise.

"Hey." She wipes off her head and shoulders with a towel and puts on a baseball cap.

"So, was that the scholarship lady?" I don't think Ez wants to talk, but I don't want to leave her when I can tell she's upset.

"Yeah." Ez lifts her hat so she can look at me. "I had to tell her what happened. How I got gassed last week, and I'm not myself."

"Good. What'd she say?"

"She said they're looking at another candidate, but they haven't made a decision yet. She said she'll take my accident into consideration."

"Okay, that's good, right?" I sit on a towel at her feet.

Ez sighs. "I don't know. They're looking at another candidate. That candidate is Charlotte, and Charlotte had a good meet. She PR'd in the 50 back and the 50 free, in which she kicked my butt, if you didn't notice."

"Eh, she beat you by half a second. It's hardly kicking your butt."

"Still. If they were to make a decision today, they'd pick her."

"But they're not. So, there's still time."

Sophie interrupts our conversation by leaning into the pop-up tent. "Hey, anyone have a tampon?"

"I do!" I grab my bag and reach for the little pocket on the inside. But when I unzip the pocket, I remember what's in there—the snow globe polar bear. I haven't thought about it in a while. The sight of it makes me itch, but I fish out a tampon and toss it to Sophie.

"Thanks, Maddie," Sophie hollers as she runs off. I

quickly zip up the pocket in my bag before the sight of the bear can make me queasy.

I stand up and reach my hand to Ez. "C'mon. Let's go watch the free relays. Owen is anchoring for our boys' Team A, and they might actually win."

"Fine." Ez takes my hand, and as we walk back to the spectator section, Aidan and Nico walk toward us.

Nico came in just before the 50 free, but I haven't talked to him yet. I'm glad he wasn't here to see my earlier races. Maybe I'm just worried about Ez, or worried about the future of the Eels, or pissed at Charlotte, or cursed by polar bears, but it wasn't my best meet either.

Nico gives me a big smile and a cute little wave, and my skin buzzes.

"Hi." We both say at the same time, and then giggle.

I think Ez rolls her eyes, but then she smiles. "Hey, we're going to watch the relays," she says to Aidan and Nico. "You coming?"

Aidan throws an arm around her shoulders, and they walk toward the pool. "We were just coming to find you two to boost the cheering section! They're all lined up—let's go!"

Aidan and Ez walk a few feet ahead. Aidan's goofy affection seems to be putting a smile on Ez's face today.

Nico slows down to walk with me. "How was Colorado?" I ask.

"Colorado was . . ." He squints in the sun. "Boring."

"Good," I say. "I mean, not good that it was boring, um . . . good that you're back."

"Yeah. It is good," he says. "But you and Ez don't look so happy."

I sigh. "It's been a rough meet."

"Yeah, Aidan filled me in on the thing with that Charlotte girl and the scholarship and the switching teams," he says. "Who knew swimming had so much drama?"

We find a spot on the side of the pool to cheer on the team. The 11–12 boys are still in the water. The 13–14 girls are next, and Owen and the 13–14 boys are coming up.

It's crowded around the pool deck, and I don't hate having to stand a little closer to Nico. He doesn't smell so much like paint anymore, but he still smells like citrus-fruit shampoo.

"Yeah, all we do is chase a black line on the bottom of a pool, but there's been drama all summer," I agree.

"All summer? You mean there was drama *before* the vandalism and the chlorine leak and the swimmer who left your team for another team without telling anyone?" His eyes widen.

"Yeah, a couple of other things." I don't want to tell him about the glass and the eggs. I want to keep everything Nico far away from everything Lucas, so I just say, "Business hadn't been great this summer already, and the vandalism and the leak made it all worse." I watch the pool. "It makes me a little worried."

Nico's quiet for a minute. Then he asks softly, "Like, worried about money?"

"Um, yeah, kind of." It's weird to tell him that.

The 13–14 girls climb on the blocks, and we yell out a few cheers.

Nico keeps talking after the starting buzzer rings. "So, what about a fundraiser? Like a party or something? That's what we always do for fundraisers. Like a potluck, you know— everyone brings a hotdish, and you collect donations. Or, like, make it a bake sale where everyone brings dessert, and then you sell it." His face lights up while he talks, and I forget we're supposed to be cheering on our team. The 13–14 girls are finishing their first relay leg.

"Um, what's a hotdish?" I have to ask.

"Oh right, it's like a casserole. Do you have those here?" He grins.

"Not in the summer." I laugh. "I guess we could do a bake sale in the clubhouse? But I like the idea of a party too."

"How about both?" he suggests.

"Oh! I know!" I grab his arm. "Let's have a dance! My brother is really good at making playlists. We could charge admission and have folks bring, like, snacks and cookies to sell." I suddenly realize I'm touching Nico's arm, and he doesn't mind.

He smiles slowly and moves his arm to take my hand, locking his fingers with mine. "Yeah, a dance. Let's have a dance."

I point to the pool with my other hand. "Oh! Our girls just lost." My heart is spinning at more hand-holding. "Shoot. Hope the boys do better."

They do. The 13–14 boys do so well that when they win their relay, it's by nearly a full pool length. Nico and I reluctantly drop hands to cheer and clap. The crowd goes wild, and it feels like Ez and our team have regained a little bit of enthusiasm.

It's not enough though. When all the relays are done and counted, we lose the meet. On the upside, no one from the Maple Grove team pulls the chlorine-leak alarm.

But I'm not really thinking about chlorine leaks. I'm not even really thinking about how disappointed everyone is that we lost the meet.

I'm too busy thinking about a dance. And citrus-fruit shampoo.

Chapter 17

It's Sunday evening at dinner before I can talk to my parents about the dance. Lexi is guarding at the pool, but Jack is home.

"So, what do you think?" I ask my family over tacos after I tell them the idea. "Everyone who comes to the club knows about the gas leak, so I think our team and the people in the neighborhood would come."

"We could do that," Dad says. "We had a dance there a couple of years ago in the clubhouse, remember? Maybe Monday, since Mondays are slow at the pool and furthest from meets?"

"Monday's tomorrow," I point out. I don't think I can be ready by then.

"Huh, yeah, so it is." Dad adds some cheese to his taco. "How about next Monday? Get through this Saturday's meet at Gold Heights? Is next Monday free, hon?"

"I'm sure it is," Mom answers. "Mondays are always free. Can you make it happen in a week, Maddie? Advertising and everything?"

"Yeah, a week's good." I'm excited my parents are agreeing to the dance. It's a good chance to show them how well I can manage stressful situations. "I'll get on the socials."

"Do that!" Dad says enthusiastically. "I love the socials!"

"And uh, who exactly is going to be DJ-ing this dance?" Jack leans forward.

I turn on my charming voice. "I was kinda hoping you would, handsome, amazing, smart, noble brother."

Jack chuckles. "Well, when you ask like that, how can I say no? And Tyler's dad has speakers we can borrow. He might even have a disco ball."

"Ew, I hate disco balls." I wrinkle my nose. "Too many flashy lights."

"Yeah, I knew you would feel that way." He throws a chip at me. "But everyone else loves 'em."

"Whatever will bring in the money." I sigh, but I'm smiling. "I'll do my best to get past it."

"So how exactly are we going to make money on this dance?" Jack asks. "Auctioning off slow dances with the DJ?"

"Gross, no." I throw an olive at him. "We'll charge admission, and maybe have a bake sale to make more money?"

"Stop throwing food. And it's too hot to bake," Mom says. "Can I make no-bake granola bars?"

"Just get the Kool Ice slushie guy," Jack says through a mouthful of taco. "He comes to our school dances. If it's a fundraiser, he'll give you a percentage or something.

Trust me, kids would rather eat slushies than their mom's brownies."

Mom nods. "Yes, do that. No baking. And I am not even the slightest bit offended by that comment."

"I'll get the number for you, Mad, and the speakers." Jack grabs another taco. "This is gonna be fun."

Every day after practice, I do something to get ready for the dance. Throwing myself into preparations makes me less nervous about how it's going to go. Mostly.

On Monday, I text the Kool Ice slushie guy. I do not like talking on the phone, so I'm relieved I don't actually have to speak to him.

The Kool Ice slushie guy confirms that he will be at the dance at seven, and he can set up in the parking lot. I check "Refreshments" off my list.

Every afternoon, I hit the socials with everything I've got. Instagram, TikTok, Snapchat. I even ask my mom to post on her Facebook account a few times to get the word out to parents. It's a pretty effective social media campaign, I think. Lots of reposts and likes and shares.

Charlotte even makes a TikTok advertising the dance. She must have gotten her phone back. No one has talked to her since the Maple Grove meet, and I'm still mad at her for abandoning our team. Maybe Charlotte is just helping advertise the dance because she feels guilty for leaving, but her dance TikTok has more than three hundred views, so that's some great advertising.

I'm trying not to think about Lucas, or his brother who wants to buy our club. But on Wednesday, I check Lucas's Instagram, and I see that he's shared one of Charlotte's posts about the dance. I hope that doesn't mean he's planning to come. I'd thought about blocking him again after the Fourth of July, but I want to know if he makes any more rude posts about our club.

Thursday afternoon, Ez and I raid the decoration cabinet at the clubhouse. We've had enough parties there over the years that we have some old streamers and other random décor.

Ez pulls out a poster of an ice cream cone and another one of a movie projector. "Can we use these? Do we have a theme or anything?"

"Nah, that one was for an ice cream social and the other was for outdoor movie night." I study the posters, then can't help but giggle. "That went horribly wrong, remember?"

Ez laughs. "Yeah, I remember your brother falling through the movie screen right at the moment when Ursula emerges from the ocean. It was terrifying! That scene is bad enough! I'm pretty sure I had nightmares for weeks."

"And that's why we don't have outdoor movie nights anymore!" I'm happy to see Ez laughing and goofing off. She seems to have her strength back and should be in good shape for the meet against Gold Heights on Saturday.

"So, no theme then?" Ez sifts through the decorations.

"I don't know. How about, 'Give us money so we don't have to sell the club and lose our swim team forever'? Does that fit on a poster?" I sigh.

"I know!" Ez pulls out a string of lights. "'Save the Eels!' You can draw big pictures of eels and we can out-line them in lights to make them 'electric'!"

"I love it!" I pull out some paint pens. "This might actually be fun *and* help us out."

"Oh, Maddie." Ez bumps my shoulder. "It's a dance. It's supposed to be fun."

"It'll be fun, as long as Lucas doesn't show up," I mumble.

"Why would he? He doesn't even live in the neigh-borhood, and after he posted that thing about the poo in the pool, he has to know people here don't like him."

"Right, but he did show up Fourth of July."

Ez snorts. "I don't think we made him feel very wel-come. I even saw Jack give Lucas a few dirty looks and tell him to walk when he wasn't even running."

"Yeah, Jack loves telling people to walk, but Lucas is not great at getting messages," I point out. "And he shared Charlotte's dance post, so we know he knows about it, and it is open to everyone. I mean, we want to make money."

"Nah, he's got to know he's not welcome." Ez waves the idea away. "No one comes to a dance hosted by the girl who rejected him a thousand times."

I clam up. What Ez says makes sense, but Lucas knows how to get to me. He might not have a reason to come to the dance, but that doesn't mean he won't.

The meet at Gold Heights on Saturday goes pretty well. Ez is definitely back to form and kills it in all of her races. But the scholarship lady isn't there to see it.

Ez's only second place comes from the medley relay. With no Charlotte, Lexi puts me on Team A again in the butterfly. Both Sophie and Jess struggle a little, so we're behind when I dive in for the fly leg. I do a decent individual time, but it's nowhere near as fast as the butterflier on the Gold Heights team. By the time Ez dives in for free, it's too far to make up, and we take second, just like at the Maple Grove meet.

I can't help but think the only difference between a first-place relay team and a second-place relay team is me.

We still end up winning the meet. The only other bummer is that the meet is away at Gold Heights, which is all the way across town. So, we don't get a lot of extra spectators, like Nico. I text with him all week but haven't seen him since the last meet.

On Friday, he'd texted:

Nico: sorry i can't make the meet
tomorrow

> Me: it's ok it's far

> Nico: but will be at dance monday with O & A
>
> save me a dance 🕺

> Me: obvs 😌

I am so excited for this dance.

The day of the dance is the kind of day where it's hot even at seven thirty in the morning. I pull shorts instead of sweats over my suit to go to practice, and I don't want to get out of the pool at nine because I can already feel the heat radiating off the concrete. The rain and cool weather before the Fourth of July weekend is a distant memory.

I'm planning to get to the dance early to make sure everything is in place. Monday afternoon, I'm standing in my room staring at my clothes. I feel a mini panic coming on trying to decide what to wear, but before it fully hits, there's a knock at my door.

It's Lexi and Kari. They've agreed to be chaperones tonight, and since they're both over eighteen, my parents said it's okay. Mom and Dad will be there, too, and a couple of other parents.

Lexi falls on my bed. "It is SO hot out. Better be sure the AC is working in the clubhouse, or it's gonna be a rough night."

"Thanks." I roll my eyes. "Give me one more thing to worry about."

Kari starts pulling things out of my closet. "Well, you're so cute, you don't have to worry about how you look."

I blush. "I can't decide what to wear."

"Wear as little as possible. It's too hot for clothes." Lexi groans.

"Yeah, I don't think that's going to work," I mumble.

"Oh! I have a thing." Lexi sits straight up. "It's a dress."

Kari glances at her. "You wear dresses? Why haven't I seen this?"

"I haven't worn it since like sophomore year. But it would be perfect on you, Mad." Lexi jogs to her room and returns with a red scrap of material.

"No way. I can't wear that—that's too hot. Like the other kind of hot." And I suddenly feel hot.

"Oh my god, it is hot." Kari holds up the dress. "Just put it on."

I go into the bathroom and put on the dress. Lexi was right; it fits perfect. But it's too much. It's made of a slippery, silky material that's fitted through the top and flares at the hips. It's short and spaghetti-strapped. It's gorgeous, but I can't imagine wearing it around people.

When I show Kari and Lexi, they fall all over themselves. "You have to wear that!" Lexi says. "That dark-haired boy won't be able to keep his eyes off of you!"

I don't mind the idea of Nico looking at me in this

dress, but I shudder at the thought that someone like Lucas might.

Lucas should be far away from this dance. I still haven't heard anything from him since the Fourth of July—he hasn't tried to message me late at night with his problems, and he's only posted that one Instagram story about the dance. I hope that means the Lucas crush saga is over, and that I never have to tell my parents about him.

I glance at the clock, realize I have to go set up in five minutes, and grab an oversized white T-shirt. I put it over the dress, tying it at the waist.

"Ah!" Kari shrieks. "Take that off."

"Maybe," I say. "But I have to go. See you there?" I grab my favorite lip gloss from my dresser and toss it in the shirt pocket.

"Madeleine Conner, you are way too hot to cover up like that!" Lexi yells at me as I hurry down the stairs.

As I burst onto the street, the sun is practically blinding. It's well over one hundred degrees out. But I have things to do. I hurry down the street, searching for the shadiest path. In the six minutes it takes to get to the clubhouse, I think I get a sunburn.

The white T-shirt is sweaty, so I take it off while I work to set up. The first thing I do is check the AC, which is blasting cool air into the event room, then I load up a couple of water jugs with ice.

It's going to be a hot night.

Chapter 18

I don't put the T-shirt back on all night. It's too hot. I don't stop moving all night either. First Ez and I collect money at the door. We've suggested a five-dollar admission, but we also have a tip jar out for Jack at the DJ station, and he's agreed to donate it to the cause.

I spend most of the first hour hustling around making sure the water jugs are full, and the Kool Ice guy is doing okay, and no one's fighting, and the decorations aren't falling down. I really want to show my parents I can handle this.

When Nico comes in with Aidan and Owen, all I want to do is dance with him, or at least talk to him, but someone knocks over the water jug, and I have to run to the closet and grab towels.

Nico comes over to me while I'm cleaning up. "Need some help?" he says.

"Help would be good." I hand him a towel. Then I look at his dark eyes and my heart flutters. "Hi."

"Hi." He grins. "So, am I going to get to dance with you tonight or are you too busy?" he says near my ear over the music, and my heart shifts from fluttering to full-on pounding.

I smile and try to act cool. "Sure. Let me just take the towels out and refill the water jug. I'll, um, be back in a few minutes."

He picks up a towel. "Can I help you with any of that?"

I don't have time to think about how he can help me without having to explain where everything is, so I blurt, "No. It's okay. Go have fun. Dance! I'll find you later."

He gives me a half smile and nods. I feel bad for not giving him attention, but I can't worry about his feelings right now—I have too much to do. Refilling the water takes a long time, and I have to search around for more ice, so when I get back to the event room, I don't see Nico anywhere.

The room is packed. I recognize most of the kids from our age group and the 15–18s, and even some 9–10s and 11–12s. It looks like people brought friends, too, because there's a handful of kids I don't recognize. They're all excited and bouncing all over the room while the music pounds and the lights flash. I'm glad everyone seems happy, but the energy is overwhelming.

One of the bounciest is Charlotte. She's wearing super-short denim shorts and a hot-pink tank, and her hair is long and flowy around her shoulders. I don't know if I'm happy to see her or not. She left our team, but she always loves a party. And she did do some great advertising for the dance.

Ez, Owen, and Aidan are dancing in a group with Sophie and Jess. Charlotte hops through them and moves on to another group. Ez has actually put on makeup, including lightly drawn eyebrows, and is wearing a flowy blue, purple, and green patterned scarf around her head and a short blue tank dress. It's really cute, and it's not quite as short as mine. I tug on the bottom of Lexi's red dress and wish it was longer.

Jack switches the music to a slow song, and I move through the room looking for Nico. Both Owen and Aidan have put their arms around Ez and each other, and they're laughing hysterically. Most of the younger kids head outside for Kool Ice. The older kids pair off, finding someone—a friend or a crush or a date (or in Ez's case, two friends)—to dance with. The room is dark, and the disco ball makes everything blurry. It's hard to focus.

When I finally see Nico, I wish I hadn't. His hands rest loosely at the waist of Charlotte's friend Tina. Her hands sit on his shoulders. Her long dark hair sways to the music, and Nico awkwardly bops his head and looks around the room.

My heart falls to my flip-flops. I duck into the kitchen area and lean my cheek against the cool metal freezer door. The music thuds against the walls, but I'm relieved to be away from the flashing. Leaning against the sink, I pull the fabric of Lexi's dress away from my skin. It feels so tight. The image of Tina and Nico dancing is burned into my brain. It's just one dance, I tell myself. They weren't very close, and he wasn't even looking at her.

And what did I expect? That he would only dance

with me? That when I'm not even around, he's just supposed to wait for me?

I take a deep breath and head back into the event room. The slow song is over. Maybe I'll get Nico's next dance. But when I see him, he's still dancing with Tina. They're not touching anymore, but Nico is smiling at her and talking and laughing.

Over her shoulder, Nico catches my eye and gives me a little wave. I think he starts to walk toward me, but then Tina turns around, sees me, and leans in to whisper something in his ear. He takes his eyes off me to respond to her, and that's it. I can't watch anymore.

Before I can figure out what to do about Nico, Ez grabs my arm and drags me into the hallway.

"Maddie! There you are! Look at this email I just got." I stare at her because the image of Nico and Tina is still in my brain, and I can't process what she's saying. "The recruiter—she'll be here at East Valley this weekend for our last meet. It's my chance to come back from the Maple Grove meet."

I pull myself together for Ez and try to form a sentence. "Um, okay, that's great."

Ez is still talking and kind of hopping around. "I just—I'm nervous. I'm nervous about not getting the scholarship. If I don't get it, I can't be on the Tomlin training team, and then I might not even get to go to Tomlin at all. We can't afford it."

"You're nervous? You're never nervous about swimming." I worry that came out a little mean sounding.

It must have, because Ez's head shifts and her eyes widen. Then they narrow. "You know, you don't have, like, a *monopoly* on anxiety just because you *have* anxiety. Other people get nervous too."

My stomach feels hollow. "I know, I just—everything is weird." I feel like I can't breathe. I pull at the red dress. "And I borrowed this dress from Lexi, and I don't know if it fits, and I just—I feel like everyone is looking at me. Everyone except Nico, the one I actually want to be looking at me. He keeps looking at Tina."

"Well, Tina keeps putting herself in his line of vision and you keep putting yourself out of the room. You look fine," Ez growls.

I pull at the bottom of the dress. "I don't—"

"Please. You're *fine*." Ez grabs the end of her scarf. "It's not like there's something about you, like, say, your *head*, that makes people stare at you all the time, so what's there to worry about?" Ez is mad now. Her face is red, and her eyes are shining. It's not unusual for Ez to get mad, but it is unusual for Ez to get mad at me.

"What's there to worry about?" I stammer. "My parents are running out of money, a guy is vandalizing our pool because of me, my dress is too tight, and everyone is looking at me like I'm going to combust?"

"Trust me, I know when people are looking," Ez says. "And I know that if everyone is looking at someone, it's the weird hairless girl who almost passed out at practice. Like, maybe I really am sick like they all think I am. They're *always* looking at me."

"No!" I blurt. "They're *not* always looking at you. You know, I might not have the *monopoly* on anxiety, but you don't have a monopoly on worrying that people look at you. Other people worry that they're being stared at too."

Ez backs away and looks at me like I slapped her. I feel like I did.

"Whatever, Maddie." She puts up her hands and ducks into the bathroom.

I don't follow her. Ez never gets mad at me. But I don't usually talk like that either. My throat tightens, and my eyes prickle like I'm going to cry. I don't know what to do, so I wander back into the dance.

But the first person I see is the person I'd somehow convinced myself wouldn't be here.

Lucas.

Chapter 19

I don't know why he's here, but the sight of him turns my stomach. He sees me as soon as I walk into the dance. He's been looking for me.

Then Jack puts on another slow song.

Lucas reaches for me. "Maddie, will you dance with me?"

I back up. I'm afraid to open my mouth because I suddenly feel like I'm going to throw up. Lucas must take my silence as a yes, because he puts his hands at my waist and leans close to me.

"I just want one more chance with you. I heard about the dance, and I knew I had to come. I knew this was my chance," he whispers in my ear. I feel like spiders are crawling over my shoulders. His breath still smells like hot dogs. Who has hot-dog breath all the time?

"I don't want . . . to dance. No chances," I squeak. I push at his arms, but he clasps them around my waist.

His hands creep up my back. "It's just one dance. C'mon, Maddie, you can at least give me that." His arms tighten around me, and I'm suddenly terrified. I can't get away from him.

"I don't . . . I don't," I say, but it comes out a whisper.

"One dance. You owe me that after accusing me of vandalizing your pool," he whispers.

That's it. Anger fills my body.

"No! Stop touching me! I don't owe you *anything*." I push on his chest, hard, until he releases his arms and stumbles backward. "And I don't want to dance with you."

Lucas stares at me, mouth open. A few people around us are staring, too, but the music still plays, pounding in my ears.

Lucas's eyes get dark like when I gave him back the snow globe. "You're so cold, Maddie. All you are is cold. Like when you gave me back the present I picked out just for you. And when you ignored my messages after I said all those, you know, personal things about my family. It's just cold."

"No, it's not!" I didn't know my voice could get that loud. "Why would you tell me personal things anyway? It's not like we're close."

"Because I want to get close to you! But you keep me in the friend zone," he whines.

"Great!" I'm yelling again. "You're not in the friend zone anymore! Because guess what? We're. Not. Friends!"

A crowd has gathered. My heart races.

"Why are you so mean to me?" Lucas looks like he's going to cry, but I know he just wants me to feel sorry for him. I wonder if his parents are really splitting up or if he just told me that to get me to be nice.

"I'm not mean!" I see Nico, who is ignoring Tina to watch me, and my throat catches. But I keep talking. "Just because I don't like you, doesn't mean you can just smash glass and leave it under a block and then eggs and ketchup and chlorine gas—"

"Wait a second." Lucas holds up his hand. "Yeah, fine. I did throw eggs at your pool. It was right after you gave me back the snow globe, and I was pissed. But I didn't do that other stuff. And once I smashed that snow globe, I never saw it again, so I don't know what you're saying about glass under a block."

"So, you did egg our pool." I fold my arms over my chest. "I knew it was you when I found the polar bear in the bushes. And you *did* smash the snow globe—you didn't drop it on accident like you said before. That's two lies."

"Yeah, I egged you. I didn't do anything else though." Lucas scowls.

I pause. Lucas admitted to the egging. That's big. But he might be telling the truth about the other stuff. Why would he confess to part of it but not all of it, unless he really didn't do it?

I take a deep breath to even out my heart rate. "Whatever, even if you didn't do those things, you still just need to leave me alone."

Lexi and Kari appear on either side of Lucas like two angels. Lexi puts a hand on Lucas's shoulder. "I think it's time for you to go, young man."

Kari grabs my hand and leans in. "You okay?"

I nod. "Actually, yeah." My anger is fading, and I just want Lucas to leave. I turn to him one more time. "Will you have to wait for a ride home or something?"

"Um, no. I came with my brother," Lucas mumbles.

"What? Why is your brother here?" I blurt.

"I don't know. He said he had business to do with your parents, and did I want to come, and I said yeah." Lucas looks defeated. Good.

Lexi still has a hand on Lucas's shoulder. "Well, then, let's go see your brother and tell him it's time to go home."

I step out into the hallway, relieved to be away from the music and the stares. Down the hall, voices ring from the office—voices that belong to my parents and someone else. I glance through the office window and see someone with a huge, muscly back and dark hair. Derek Bryce.

Lexi, Kari, Lucas, and I stand in the hallway, and when we hear that they're talking about the future of the club, Lexi's hand drops from Lucas's shoulder and her face crumples. I didn't even realize Kari was still holding my hand until she drops it to take Lexi's.

Jack comes running down the hallway. "Um, what's going on?"

"Shh!" Lexi whispers.

"Oh, are we eavesdropping?" Jack covers his mouth. "I saw a bit of a tussle with my little sister, and I'm check-ing it out," he whispers as he glares at Lucas.

Lucas drops his head and walks slowly down the

hall, bleached hair falling in his eyes. Jack and I follow him, moving out of earshot of the office.

"I'm fine." I nod. "But who's DJ-ing?"

"I left your friend Aidan in charge of the playlist and the equipment. I like that kid. But I don't know if I like this kid." He points at Lucas. "I remember him from the Fourth of July. It seems like he does not know the rules."

"What rules?" I keep my voice low. "I didn't know there were rules."

"You know, *rules*. The rules about how when you ask a girl to dance and she says no, you don't dance with her. And when a girl is pushing you away, it means stop touching her." Jack keeps his eyes on Lucas. "I mean, this is first-grade stuff, dude."

Lucas continues staring silently at the ground. I think he's going to cry. But he nods his head a tiny bit, like maybe he's actually getting the message. Obviously, Lucas wasn't listening to me when I told him I wasn't interested, but he listens to a guy like Jack. Just one more reason Lucas would not make a good boyfriend: he doesn't listen to girls. My face burns with anger.

"Also, sorry I didn't get to you sooner, Mad." Jack puts a hand on my shoulder. "By the time I realized what was going on, you had it handled."

"It's cool." I exhale and smile at my brother. "I did handle it, huh?" I wish my parents had seen how well I handled it.

"Yeah, you did." Jack's voice lifts. "So what are we doing in the hallway?"

Kari and Lexi have their ears to the office door.

"Shush it!" Lexi demands. "This is the important part."

Jack and I go silent and move closer to our sister. Lucas stands awkwardly against the wall. We hear my dad from inside the office. He doesn't know we're listening.

"So, to clarify, with this offer, we still manage the club?" Dad asks.

"Yep," says a voice I'm pretty sure belongs to Derek. "We'll find positions for both you and your wife. And your children can still be lifeguards, even with no swim team."

My dad sighs heavily. "I guess we don't have a choice. We just can't recoup our losses, and it's only getting worse. And if we don't update the locker rooms and replace that tile, the county will close us down anyway."

What? I thought the dance was doing well! There's a ton of kids here. I look at my sister and am glad Kari's holding on to her so she doesn't fall over.

I do the math to try to figure out where I went wrong. Even if there are a hundred kids here, at five dollars each, that's only five hundred dollars. And even if Jack's tip jar and the Kool Ice guy bring in a couple hundred each, we're still under a thousand dollars. It's not enough to keep a business running or pay for new tile or a new chlorination system, or pay for anything, really. It's nowhere near the ten thousand dollars my parents need to make the repairs to pass the inspection.

I should have known I couldn't raise ten thousand dollars in one night. I wonder if my parents knew and just let me have the dance to make me feel good. I don't. I feel mad and ridiculous.

Tears prick my eyelids, and I lean my head against the wall. In the office, my mom mumbles something I can't hear.

Derek's voice sounds disgustingly happy as he opens the office door. "Great! I'll bring the final papers by in the morning." He catches sight of the five of us in the hallway. "Oh, hey, bro. Ready to go?"

Kari clears her throat and speaks for all of us. "Oh, he's ready."

Derek throws an arm around his brother. "Have a good time?" Clearly Derek has no idea what just happened in the dance.

I watch Derek and Lucas walk down the hallway and out the main clubhouse door, and I know if I don't get out of here, I might actually pass out. I push past Lexi and run the opposite direction. I don't think anyone follows me, but I really don't know, because I don't turn around. I run through the girls' locker room and out onto the pool deck.

The air hits me like an open oven, but at least it's quiet. I walk away from the building, away from the music and the flashing lights. I wander all the way over to the pool, kick off my flip-flops, and step onto the first step of the pool, just under the surface. The water cools my skin, and I breathe more evenly.

Sitting on the edge of the pool with my feet dangling in the water, I turn everything over in my head. My parents are selling the pool because we can't pay for updates and repairs. I can't even believe that's true, but it's been building all summer. It shouldn't be a surprise.

And then there's Nico. I know that him dancing with Tina doesn't necessarily mean he likes her. At our middle school dances, everyone kind of danced with everyone—they didn't have to really *like* them. I even danced with Lucas a couple of times, to be nice.

But if I wasn't sure how I felt about Nico, I am now. Thinking of him dancing with Tina makes my stomach hurt. I know I like him, and not just because he's new. I like Nico because he listens to me, and he asks what book I'm reading, and he's observant and interesting and nice and smells like oranges and says words like "hotdish."

I think about that night I thought he was going to kiss me. I really hope that wasn't the only time he'll look like he might kiss me. I really hope sometime he actually kisses me. I think he would have soft lips and not-stinky breath.

Hopefully, my scene with Lucas didn't make Nico afraid of me. Blowing up at Lucas, telling him everything I've been holding in, was like coming up for air after swimming a full lap without a breath. I never knew I could feel so relieved just by yelling. My throat hurts, but it was worth it.

Pulling my phone out of my pocket, I wish for a text from Nico.

I get it. He says:

> Nico: i think i messed up where r u

Okay. So, he's probably not afraid of me. And I was the one who told him to have fun and dance. I can't be mad at him for dancing.

I don't text him back right away. I'm not sure what to say yet.

There are also a few texts from Ez. One of my favorite things about being best friends with Ez is that she doesn't stay mad for long.

> Ez: omg sorry i was super upset but
>   come back are you ok?

> where are you? lexi said some stuff
>   went down but wont let me go
>   outside

> she said no kids at the pool until

> dance is over

> also she seems upset

I do text Ez back.

> Me: i'm sorry too coming back in
>   now

While I'm debating what to text Nico, a long text from him comes in:

Nico: ok i can't find you and i have to tell you i didn't really want to dance with tina she asked me to dance and i said i was waiting for you and she was just like ok well let's just dance until she comes back and threw her hands on my shoulders and i didn't really know what to do but i probably should have done something different and i saw you yell at that kid and i hope you're ok

Me: wow that's a really long text

Nico: yeah i just wanted you to know also sorry

are you coming back? are you ok?

I do want to go in and see if there's still time for a dance with Nico, but I have to talk to Ez first. She's upset, and she should be. What I said was mean, and I have to apologize to my best friend before I can do anything else.

Me: yeah but i have to take care of something first

I also have to talk to my parents about what's been happening with Lucas. Maybe if I tell them about Lucas, it'll give them some kind of clue about who caused all the vandalism. I step out of the pool, slide into my flip-flops, and head back to the dance by way of the girls' locker room.

Before going in, I detour by the chlorine tanks. Dad has put a padlock on the gate, and I pull it gently to make sure it holds. I run my hand along the boards enclosing the tanks, and I even inspect the bushes along the fence that forms the back border of the tanks. I just can't see how someone could have gotten into the tanks without anyone noticing.

Then I see it.

The disco lights from inside catch on something shining in the blackberry bushes right behind the chlorine tanks. I really hope it's not glass again. The sun is setting, and the evening is getting dark. It's hard to see what I'm looking at. I think about finding the polar bear in the bushes after the egging and wonder if whoever set off the chlorine alarm left a clue behind too.

I lean closer. The disco ball lights are definitely highlighting something solid in the bushes, but it's not glass. It's metal. I try to push aside the branches, but the thorns prick my hands. Whatever it is that's catching the light, it's buried so deep in the bushes behind the tanks that no one could get it out without scratching up their arms. I look at it again. It's not metal. It's pink metallic, like the cap of a shaving cream bottle.

Charlotte's shaving cream bottle.

Chapter 20

It all suddenly falls into place. It wasn't Lucas. It was Charlotte. Charlotte never got in the water the day of the leak—because she knew the alarm would go off. Charlotte has a new puppy that she takes for walks, and she probably has to clean up his poop. Maybe she even brought the snow globe glass to the pool—she kept asking if everyone was okay that day. I have to find Charlotte. I have to find out why she would vandalize our pool.

But first, I have to find Ez. I run through the locker room and into the clubhouse.

Ez is right there, pacing the hallway. "Maddie! Where were you? I know I was mad, but I'm sorry, and I heard Lucas was here and he confessed to the egging and you yelled at him? I can't believe I missed it!"

"It's okay, really. I'm sorry too. But I have to show you something." I pull Ez into the locker room.

"Okay, but I just want to explain." Ez tugs on the end of her scarf.

"Explain what?" I barely even remember that we had a fight. "You don't have to explain. I was anxious, and I got mean. I'm sorry, really, but come with me. You have to see this." I motion for her to follow me.

Ez keeps talking as I lead her through the locker room. "It's okay. It's me, really. It's just this scholarship gets me so worked up. I feel like I need to get the scholarship so people don't always think of me as the girl with no hair. I want to at least be the girl with no hair who swims amazingly."

I stop at the door between the locker room and the pool. Ez lost her hair so long ago that I sometimes forget it's something she has to deal with all the time.

"Trust me," I tell my best friend. "People don't just think of you as the girl with no hair *or* as the girl who swims amazingly. I mean, they think that, too, but you also get to be friends with people and have fun, you know? Do you even know how much fun Aidan and Owen have with you? Not just tonight but at every meet and practice? I mean, sometimes I even forget you don't have hair. I bet lots of your friends do."

"Really?"

"Really. But now I really, *really* have to show you something." I grab Ez's hand, pull her over to the bushes behind the tanks, and point at the shaving cream cap.

She stares at the bushes. "What am I looking at?" She leans over and looks deeper. "Ohhhh! That's Charlotte's! It's the cap to the shaving cream bottle she was using. Why is it here by the tanks?"

"I think . . . I think Charlotte dropped it. Not recently,

but a while back. It's dirty like it's been there a while. And it has water spots like it's been rained on."

I watch Ez's face as she follows my thoughts. "A while back . . . as far back as the leak?"

I nod.

Ez takes a closer look. "And no one, like the police or your dad, saw it?"

"Nope. Or if they did, they thought it was trash. It's buried so deep in the bushes it just looks like garbage. I only saw it because the disco light was shining on it." I point to the window of the event room behind us. "So I think what it means is . . ."

"Charlotte turned the knob? Charlotte did it! Oh. My. God." Ez pulls at the ends of her colorful scarf. "Does this mean she did everything? Except the eggs, because Lucas just said he did that, but everything else?"

"Well, I don't know if it's enough proof, but yeah, I think this is evidence."

"Why though?" Ez looks at me with scrunched eyes. "Why would Charlotte sabotage our team? How could she do that to us?"

"I don't know. But she has been weird all summer," I remind her. "Oh! And her arm was scratched the day of the leak. She said it was her puppy, but I bet it was the bushes. Something is definitely up with her."

"I'm gonna find out what it is." Ez storms off into the locker room. "Stay here! Don't let anyone touch those bushes!"

A minute later she comes back out, pulling Charlotte behind her.

Charlotte is still giddy from the dance. She's holding a cup of pink Kool Ice that matches her shirt. "Is this going to be fast? I want to go back in. Tyler looks so cute tonight!"

"I don't think it's going to be fast," I say. I point to the bushes.

Charlotte giggles, but her eyes dart around like she doesn't want to look at us. "What's in there? This is weird. You're kind of creeping me out."

"Just look right here," I say. "And tell me what you see."

"Ew, no, those bushes are super prickly." Charlotte pulls away from Ez's grasp. She's not giggling anymore.

I grab her arm and point to the now-faded scratch. "You would know, wouldn't you?"

Charlotte's face changes. She knows we know. She doesn't look into the bushes because she knows what's there. She looks from my angry face to Ez's angry face and then covers her face with her hands.

"I tried to get that annoying cap out of the bushes, but I couldn't reach it," Charlotte whispers. "I didn't think anyone would see it."

"Well, thanks to the shiny disco lights, and Maddie's good eye for finding things in bushes, we did see it," Ez grumbles. "And we know it's yours."

"You did all of it, didn't you?" I step closer to Charlotte. "I mean, not the eggs, but the glass on the pool deck, the ketchup . . . the code brown was your new puppy's, wasn't it? You wanted practice to get canceled." I sound mean again, but unlike when I sounded mean at Ez, this time it's justified.

Ez steps closer too. Charlotte looks around like she might run away.

"Why, Charlotte?" Ez says. "To sabotage my chances at the Tomlin training scholarship so you could get it yourself?"

Charlotte takes her hands from her face, and tears fall down her cheeks.

"Or is it because you knew you were switching teams and wanted your new team to beat us?" I put my hands on my hips.

"No!" Charlotte sobs. "I didn't want to switch teams. That was my parents. All my parents. I don't want to win. And I don't even want to be on the Tomlin training team or go there for high school."

"What?" Ez takes a step back, pulling the scarf off her head.

"I want my last year of middle school to be normal. I don't want to be swimming all the time. Or at all, really. I just want to finish eighth grade and then go to East Valley High with everyone else." Charlotte sits down on the pavement, right where she is.

"Then why? *Why* did you mess up our pool?" I sit down next to her. I guess she's not going to run. Ez paces behind us, wringing her scarf in her hands. She's not ready to sit down.

Charlotte pulls her knees into her chest. "I didn't mean to hurt anyone," she says. "I just wanted to do things that would close the pool. Then later, when I did bad at meets and didn't get the scholarship, I could blame it on the canceled practices and stress."

Ez pauses. "Couldn't you just tell your parents you didn't want to swim anymore?"

"I tried." Charlotte wipes a tear from her chin. "But they wouldn't listen. They said swimming would get me into the best high school, then the best college. College! I'm not even done with middle school yet! Then they said if I didn't swim on the Tomlin training team, they'd take my phone and cancel my TikTok account."

"That's harsh," I say. For Charlotte and her fifteen thousand followers, her phone is everything. But I'm still mad. That's not an excuse for doing horrible things.

"You have no idea, Maddie." Charlotte meets my eyes. "You have nice parents. But for mine, it's all about what I did wrong and what I can do better. It's every day. All the time. Everything. Better, better, better. They even took my phone when I switched teams because I was like five minutes late to my first day of practice. I couldn't post, and I lost like a thousand followers in one day."

"So what do you want to do, if you don't swim?" I ask. "You've always been a swimmer."

"Yeah, I like swimming because I like winning. It's not a surprise that I like attention." Charlotte stares at the pool. "But all the TikToks, all the social media—it made me love being in front of a camera. I want to act, do theater, be in plays and musicals at the public high school. Tomlin doesn't even have a drama department or do musicals or anything like that."

I can't help thinking how different Charlotte and I are. "But your parents——"

"Say there's no future in acting. No scholarships, no special treatment like I could get with swimming." Charlotte hangs her head.

"Okay, sure, I mean, that sucks." Ez paces again. "But that's not a good reason to hurt people and vandalize the pool."

"I know," Charlotte says. "But I couldn't not win, or make it look like I wasn't trying. My parents would have known. I just thought if I didn't do as well at meets, I could blame it on our bad practices. I never wanted anyone to get hurt."

"But people did get hurt," I say. "Not just Ez. Lexi fell on the ketchup, and while my parents didn't get hurt, it cost a lot of money to make sure the glass and everything got out of the pool." I fold my arms over my chest. I'm softening to Charlotte a tiny bit, probably because she's crying so hard, but I am not ready to forgive her.

Charlotte shudders when she takes a deep breath. "The glass. The glass was what started it. I didn't plan it or anything. I was mad at my mom for making me go to practice on the last day of school. I wanted to hang out with my friends at Tina's house. She was having a party, and we had like three dances we wanted to work on and post on my TikTok."

"And it had to be your account. You had to be in the middle of it." Ez rolls her eyes.

"Yeah, it had to be my account. I have the following. And also, I just didn't want to practice. It was the last day of school!" Charlotte's jaw tenses. "So, on my way out of school, I saw a couple pieces of broken glass in a garbage can. I don't know where they came from, but I know coaches freak out when there's glass on the deck. I thought maybe I could make it so practice was canceled, and I could go to Tina's."

"Wait. You didn't even know the glass was from the snow globe Lucas gave me?" My face feels hot.

"Lucas gave you a snow globe? That's super weird," Charlotte says.

"That doesn't matter now." I wave it off. "I just—you know how bad it is to have glass around a pool."

A tear drops down Charlotte's cheek. "I know, I know. That's why when I got to practice, I put it under the block. I chickened out, and I thought I could just leave it there and get it later."

"If you chickened out, why didn't you just throw the glass away?" I ask. "Why leave it there for me to find?"

Charlotte takes a deep breath. "Because Lexi was standing right by the garbage can, but her back was to the blocks. I panicked. And I didn't think we'd use lane one to race. I didn't think Lexi would have other people racing with us."

"Yeah, you didn't think," Ez says. "You're lucky Maddie found it, and no one got cut."

"I know. It wasn't smart." Charlotte glances to the blocks. "But we did the race toward the beginning of practice, and as soon as Lexi saw the glass, she made us go home. It turns out I got to go to Tina's party after all."

"Wait, were you trying to skip practice because of parties or because you wanted to blame us for making you not get the scholarship?" I ask. I'm getting mad again.

Charlotte sighs. "That day was what gave me the idea to sabotage practice. But at that point, yeah, I just wanted to go to a party, so sue me for wanting to be a normal kid on the last day of school."

"You're not helping yourself," Ez fumes.

"And it wasn't just that one night," I say. "My dad had to get the vacuum repairman out to make sure there was no glass in the pool, and we couldn't open for rec swim the next morning. It cost my parents so much money."

Charlotte wipes her face. "I'm sorry, Maddie. I didn't know it would be that bad."

"And then we got egged," I say. "But we know that wasn't you, because Lucas just said it was him."

"Yeah, I heard that," Charlotte says. "And that day, I heard Lexi say that if one of the eggs had broken in the pool, we would have had to cancel practice. So, I knew if I wanted practice canceled, I had to get something gross actually in the pool."

"But did it have to be a code brown and ketchup and what you wrote?" I am not ready to accept her apology. "I mean, that's just gross. And really, really mean."

Charlotte takes a deep breath. "I got home from the pool that Wednesday night when we were all hanging out, remember?" Charlotte looks down and traces the concrete with her finger. "I had all these comments from my last post to respond to, but my mom made me walk the puppy. I was walking past the pool with the little doggie baggie, and all of a sudden, I was like, 'I know how to get out of practice tomorrow.'"

"That was a lot of work just to get out of practice," I say. I still can't believe it was Charlotte and not Lucas.

"I know. Lemme explain." Charlotte shudders. "At first, I just wanted to throw the poo in the pool. But the gate was locked."

"Yeah, to keep people out at night," Ez snarls.

"Sorry, yeah. And I knew I couldn't throw far enough to get it in the pool. I learned that from the eggs—how the fence is higher over the pool. So, I went around to the clubhouse and tried the door. It was locked too."

"But not very well." I groan.

"I just pushed it, kind of hard, and it broke. I swear I didn't know it would be that easy. I was like, 'Okay, I'll just throw in the poo and go.' But then I walked past the Snack Shack and saw the big tubs of ketchup and stuff, and I thought that would even be better. Really, I was just going to put some in the pool. But then I was holding two ketchups and the nacho cheese and the puppy's leash—"

"And you dropped them," I conclude. "Those tubs are super heavy."

"Yeah. They just slid out of my hands, and it all went everywhere."

"That doesn't explain why you wrote the words. I mean, we know we don't suck, but no one likes to see that." Ez keeps twisting her scarf.

"Right." Charlotte rubs her eyes. "So, after I dropped everything, I thought I had to make it look like a prank. Like another team did it or something."

"It looked like it took lots of work to spread out all those condiments," I remember. "I thought it was another team because it should have taken like six people to make that mess."

Charlotte groans. "No, just one puppy. He got loose and thought it was a party made for him. I had to wash him in the pool, which is how most of the ketchup that was in the pool actually got there. Yeah, it was a mess."

"Charlotte. That's so gross. And so, so harsh," I say. "And Lexi got hurt. I mean, it was a big deal."

"I know." Charlotte's crying again. "I didn't want anyone to get hurt. I just wanted it to look like a prank. I felt bad after I did it, but I couldn't take it back."

"So that's why you threw away the tubs. Cleaning up your guilt, huh?" I roll my eyes. "So, are you doing this kind of stuff at your new pool, now? You know, so you don't have to practice there either?"

Charlotte shakes her head. "No. I'm serious now. I really didn't want to hurt anyone else. After the leak, I wanted to take it all back. I'm done. I mean, I did this so my parents would go easier on me, and instead they made it harder by putting me on a team that's far away and where I don't know anybody. My plan completely failed. But I've been on time to practice and meets and races so at least I have my phone back."

"Okay, okay. Your plan failed, your phone is back, whatever, don't care," Ez says. She still hasn't sat down. "Let's talk about the chlorine leak. We know you did it. I saw you use shaving cream with that exact pink cap."

Charlotte cries harder, but then she takes a deep inhale and her story spills. "That morning, I was kind of early, so no one was around, and I saw that there was a little space between the fence and the bushes."

"Yeah, there is a little space, but it's covered in thorns, so no one should be able to get through it," I point out.

"I know," Charlotte continues. "But I used my bag to push aside the branches, peeked in at the tanks, and saw the knobs. And I'd heard that all you have to do to set off the alarm is just turn the top knob and let a little gas out."

"You knew how to set off a chlorine alarm because Lucas wouldn't shut up about it." I groan. "I can't stand him."

"Yeah, he wasn't in on it though," Charlotte says. "So, I just leaned in and twisted the knob. I didn't know it would release so much gas. I just thought it would be a little bit—that's what Lucas said, that just a little would set off the alarm. I swear, I didn't mean for Ez to get hurt. I didn't even know it would do that."

"Well, I did get hurt," Ez huffs. "You really messed up my shot at the scholarship."

"I swear, I didn't know." Charlotte sobs. "Lucas said it was no big deal."

"And you believed him. That was your first mistake. Lucas is a liar," I say, knowing how true it is. "I still can't believe you managed to get your arm past the thorns."

"I know. I was twisting around." Charlotte inhales deeply to calm her sobs. "After the shaving cream bottle got dented in the shower that day, the cap never fit on right, so it just fell out of my bag and I couldn't reach it."

"I can't believe it," a voice sounds from behind us. We turn toward the locker room, and Lexi emerges from the shadows. "I can't believe one of my swimmers would do something like that. This night just keeps getting weirder."

"How much did you hear?" I ask. It's hard to see Lexi's expression with the sun almost down, but I can hear the anger in her voice.

"Enough," Lexi says. "You're not supposed to be out here, you know. But I was worried about you, Maddie, when I didn't see you for a while after that weird thing with that Lucas kid. And then . . ."

"Please don't tell my parents yet." Charlotte can barely get the words out through her sobs. "Please. I know you have to turn me in, but let me make it right first."

"This is serious, Charlotte," Lexi says. "The police ruled the leak an accident, but the fallout kept people away from the pool and made families leave the team. We have to tell people it wasn't our fault."

"Just—just give me until morning." Charlotte is crying so hard she can barely talk.

Lexi sighs. "Fine. I have to think about how to handle this. You have until tomorrow's practice or I tell your parents for you. And my parents. And everyone else's parents too."

"Thank you." Charlotte tries to compose herself.

Tina appears at the locker room door. Apparently, she was able to detach herself from Nico. "Char?" she says. "We have to go. Dance is over. What's wrong?"

Charlotte wipes her face and stands. "Um, I'll tell you later. Let's go." Then she turns to Lexi and pleads, "Tomorrow, I promise."

Lexi glares and says nothing.

I glance at my phone. It's a little after nine. I guess I never got that dance with Nico after all. But as Charlotte and Tina walk out the pool gate into the night, I hear Tina say, "That Nico guy is cute, but he just left without saying goodbye. No number or anything."

I have to smile for the first time since the water jug spilled.

Chapter 21

I wake up early the next morning to my mom's voice in the kitchen. The events of the dance flood back to me, and I grab my phone. It's full of texts and notifications about some kind of confessional from Charlotte, a lot of *have you seen it??? and omg and i can't believe she did that!!!*—some from Ez, but also from Owen, Aidan, Jess, Sophie, and a handful of other kids from the team who I don't really hang out with.

There's also a text from Nico saying he's still sorry about the dance and wants to meet me soon, if I still want to see him. My heart flutters at the idea of seeing him, but I'll have to reply later. There's too much else going on.

From all the notifications, it sounds like Charlotte posted something pretty significant. I scroll to her TikTok, and there she is, all seriousness, no cap and goggles this time. It's a one-minute video confessing to causing the chlorine leak and the other vandalism incidents at the East Valley pool. She even connects to a YouTube video with a longer confession and more details. In both videos, she says she's setting up a crowdfund to help the East Valley pool recover the money her actions cost.

I'm pretty impressed with her honesty, but what's more impressive is that when I click through to the crowdfund, I see she's already raised almost a thousand dollars. It's a good start, but I don't know if it's going to save us. One thousand dollars is a long way from ten thousand.

When I come down to the kitchen, both of my parents are sitting at the table with steaming cups of coffee in front of them, along with a stack of papers and their phones.

"You saw it?" I ask.

Mom nods.

"We saw it," Dad says. "I'm sorry I didn't believe you when you said the glass and the vandalism incidents were connected to the leak."

"It's okay." I look at them both sipping coffee and trying to act calm. "But there's something else, isn't there."

"Sit down, Maddie," Mom says.

"But I'm going to be late for practice."

Dad smiles. "It's okay. I happen to know the coach, and I told her you might be late."

If they're letting me be late to practice, it must be important.

"We know you heard us talking to Derek last night," Mom says.

My heart falls, and I sit at the table across from them. "You're selling the pool. I know."

"Well, not yet," Dad says. "Charlotte's confession and the crowdfund may change things. We haven't canceled the deal yet, but we haven't signed the papers yet either. We asked Derek for another week to decide. If Charlotte can really raise ten thousand dollars, we can get new tile and pass our inspections."

A glimmer of hope leaps in my fallen heart. "Okay," I say. "You're not going to, like, have Charlotte arrested or something, are you? I mean, she really, really messed up, but I don't want her to go to jail."

Mom shakes her head. "No, we think the video was a pretty good apology. And we're working out an arrangement to have her do some community service."

I nod. "Good."

"That's not what I really want to talk to you about though." Mom sets her coffee down.

My heart pounds. I know it's time to tell my parents. "You want to know about Lucas, right?"

Mom nods. "Right. I don't know the whole story, but we know Lucas acted inappropriately with you last night, and we know he egged the pool. Because of that, we made it clear to both Lucas and Derek that Lucas is not welcomed at East Valley anymore. But I think there's more to the story."

"There is." I take a deep breath and rub the sleep out of my eyes. I tell my parents everything—from Lucas's crush two years ago, to the snow globe, to every message and text this summer, even the one where he asked me out again.

When I finish, my parents are quiet for a minute. Dad's jaw tenses. "I really don't like that kid."

"Yeah, me too," I mumble.

Mom's eyes are wet. "I'm sorry you had to go through that. But honey, when a boy is bothering you like that, you have to tell us. It sounds like he made unwanted advances toward you even after you told him no. That's sexual harassment."

I never thought about it like that. I don't really know what "advances" means, but I can kind of figure it out. I do know that what Lucas was doing wasn't something I wanted, and he knows it too.

"Should I have kept the snow globe?" I ask my parents. "Sometimes I think if I'd just kept it, none of this would have happened."

Mom takes a deep breath. "No. You did the right thing. Honey, he didn't give that to you because he cares about you and thought you would like it. He gave it to you because he wanted your attention and couldn't accept that you weren't going to give it to him freely. I'm actually really proud of you for giving it back. You were honest with him."

I can't believe everything with Lucas might actually be over. "Yeah, that's what I meant when I gave it back—to be honest. He just wasn't getting it."

"Because he wasn't actually listening to you," Dad says. "I'm proud of you too."

"We're going to call the school when it opens for fall registration—to make sure they know about his behavior and don't put you in classes together." Mom adds, "I wish you'd told us sooner so we could have helped."

I take a deep breath. "I wanted to tell you sooner, but every time something intense comes up, you're always worried it's going to make me anxious, that I won't be able to manage my anxiety. But I can. I knew I could handle it, but you don't think I can handle anything."

Mom looks stunned. She glances to Dad and back to me.

"You're right," she says with a sigh. "I hadn't realized how well you're handling your anxiety lately. With all this going on, I just thought . . . I thought it would get worse. But it's not."

I nod. "I know."

"I'm sorry I didn't trust you to handle things. And we're also sorry we kept so much from you," Mom says. "We should have talked to you about the vandalism, and about selling the club."

I smile. "Yeah, you should have. But thanks."

Dad looks me in the eye. "We *are* proud of how you're handling your anxiety. But you need to come to us if things get out of control or if you're feeling unsafe. It sounds like Lucas was getting out of control."

"Yeah, okay. I will," I say. "I promise I'll come to you if things are out of control, or even just intense."

"Good." Mom puts a hand on her heart. "And we promise to trust you to manage your anxiety, and to keep you in the family loop in the future."

I nod. That feels like a real promise this time.

When I get to the pool, no one is in the water. I'm suddenly nervous, like what if something else happened? But I realize everyone's just talking about Charlotte's video.

Lexi hollers, "Okay, team! In the water, let's go!" But she doesn't seem like she cares about practice today.

Ez rushes over to me. "Look! I just got a text from Charlotte." She shows me her phone.

> **Charlotte:** i told tomlin I don't want to be on the training team

> and i don't want the scholarship

> my parents don't like it but even they said

> it was the right thing to do

"That's great! That means it's yours, right?" I slough off my sweatshirt and get my cap and goggles out.

Ez shrugs. "I think it just means she's no longer competing for it—I still have to do well Saturday."

"Well, then, I guess we better practice." I nudge her as we get in the water to warm up.

After practice, I unzip the little pocket in my bag and pull out the tiny polar bear from the snow globe. As I walk through the gate, I drop it in the garbage can, watch it fall under food wrappers and dirty napkins, and promise myself I'll never let it bother me again.

I'm so glad our last meet of the season is at home.

The day is sunny and hot, but not as hot as it was at the dance. Once again, the breakfast sandwich smell competes with the chlorine smell, but it will never win.

When I get out of the pool after warm-ups, Lexi is at my side. "I've made some switches in the relays. Jess wants to try swimming fly, and her fly times are good."

I towel off my face. "So, I'm doing fly on Team B?" I'm oddly disappointed. I thought I liked swimming on no-pressure Team B, but I have to admit it was nice to swim on a relay team that actually had a shot at winning.

Lexi has a bit of a sparkle in her eye. "Nope, I'm putting you on Team A in breast. After the last meet, your individual best time in 50 breast is only point-one seconds behind Jess's, and her fly time is point-five seconds faster than yours. It makes sense to put her in at fly and you in at breast. Sophie and Ez will stay in back and free."

I smile. I like the idea of swimming breast in the relay much better than the noisy butterfly. Team A still makes me a little nervous, but I'll be the second leg, so there's plenty of time for Jess and Ez to make up any time I lose. And I actually like swimming breast. I know I can do it.

"Thanks, Lex." I stretch out my arms.

"Hey, don't thank me. It's just about the numbers, and you've got 'em. You can do it, Mad." She squeezes my shoulder and moves on to organize the next relay.

I barely have time to think about it because the medley is the first event. Lexi's switch was a good choice. We take first by an entire second. It feels good to think I helped Ez keep her winning record, but it also feels good just to win.

Ez nails every race, and at the end of the day, there's no question who won the meet or who's getting the scholarship. If there was a question, it's answered by the grin on Ez's face after she talks to the scholarship lady.

"Did you get it?" I ask when she hurries over to me as I clean up the 13–14 pop-up.

"Yeah! Well, not officially—she still has to talk to the committee," Ez says. "But she said it's mostly her decision and she'll be emailing later with an official offer."

"I knew you could do it." I give her a quick hug. I'm so happy for her. She's worked so hard. "I'm glad we have one more year of middle school before we go to separate high schools though."

"Eh." Ez shrugs. "Maybe we'll go to different schools for four years, but we're never not gonna be best friends."

"True. I mean, we do live on the same street."

"I'm gonna go now. Look who's coming." Ez points across the grassy area at the tall, dark-haired boy coming toward me with a shy smile on his face. I've texted with Nico all week, but I haven't seen him since the dance.

But before I can, another boy intercepts. It's Jack. He squares off in front of me. "Okay, yeah, I do see that the boy you like is coming over here, but I have to tell you something first." He hops up and down like a little kid.

"You keep forgetting he has an actual name. And make it quick." I roll my eyes, but I can tell that Jack is happy about something, and I'm excited to hear it.

"His name is Quick?" Jack scratches his head ironically.

"Oh my god, hurry up, dude!" I punch Jack in the arm.

"His name is Dude? Wow, he really owns it."

"Jack!"

"Okay, okay. Here goes." He pauses for drama. "Mom just told me that Charlotte's crowdfund worked. There's enough for locker room renovations and a new chlorination system and maybe even a new pretzel warmer."

"What? That's amazing!" I jump up and down. "She actually raised ten thousand dollars?"

"Well, I think she got to like, seven thousand and her parents kicked in two thousand. I think they felt guilty."

"Um, that's only nine thousand?" I'm suddenly worried that Jack forgot how to do math.

"And the last thousand came from, wait for it . . . the dance!" Jack does a little cheerleader move and pumps his fist in the air.

"What? I only came up with like five hundred in

admission sales and the Kool Ice guy only gave us one-fifty." Now I'm starting to worry that I forgot how to do math.

Jack grins. "And I had over three hundred in my tip jar."

"You did?" I give Jack a hug. I can't believe it actually worked. The dance, the crowdfund, everything.

"Yep," Jack says. "These kids turned out to be super generous. You probably should have charged more for admission."

"Next time." I smile. "So, we're not selling the pool?"

"We're not selling the pool. Now go get your man." Jack gives me fist bump, and I turn to Nico, who probably heard everything he said. I'm trying not to be nervous about that.

Nico smiles slowly. "Who is this man you have to get?"

"Um, no one, don't listen to my brother." I blush.

"So, can I walk you home, or hang out, or something?" he asks.

I glance around. There's still so much cleanup to do, and since it's our last meet of the season, and a home meet that we just won, the team is celebrating—like, full-on singing and dancing celebrating. "Um, I think we're having a party, actually. Can you stay? I have to clean up a little, but it should be fun."

Nico half smiles. "Okay. But is it okay if I follow you around this time? I kept trying to get your attention at the dance, but you were so busy. I didn't want to bother you, and then Tina wanted to dance, and I think I should have said no, because I really wanted to dance with you, but I couldn't find you."

He's already explained this to me in texts, but it's cute that he wants to keep explaining.

"It's okay," I tell him. And it is okay. I don't need more explanation. "I was a little all over the place that night. I don't blame you for dancing with someone who asked."

I take his hand, and we move under the 13–14 pop-up that was vacated a minute ago when half the team cannonballed into the pool and the other half stood on the side and cheered them on.

"Don't you want to jump in the pool and celebrate with your team?" he says, but he doesn't take his eyes from me. His hand is a little sweaty, but I don't mind. Mine probably is too.

"Too loud. I like quiet." I keep staring at his eyes. He's really so cute.

"Right. I knew that. So, um . . . what else do you like?" His voice is a little shaky. He leans his head down, closer to mine.

"Um, you?" I cringe. "Oh my god, that sounded cheesy."

He laughs. "No way. That's basically exactly what I was hoping you would say."

Then Nico takes my other, also sweaty hand, leans in, and kisses me lightly on the lips. My heart flutters into a million butterfly kicks, and I kiss him back. I don't even feel weird or awkward about it, probably because I imagined it in my head so much that it just feels right.

"Do you know that you smell like oranges?" I whisper, eyes still closed. I don't know why I'm talking when the cutest boy just kissed me. Maybe my chattiness has returned. I guess I do just like talking to him.

He lets out a nervous giggle. "My mom bought this orange-scented shampoo to help me get used to the idea of living in California. You know, oranges are kind of a California thing."

"Hm. Yeah, kind of. Is it working?" I open my eyes a tiny bit. "The getting used to living here thing?"

"Um, yep. It's working." He's still grinning.

As I gather the courage to go in for another kiss, Aidan pops his head under the pop-up. "Are you two making out? Aw! I love love!" Then he rushes out, and I hear, "Owen! Guess what?"

"Ignore them." Nico grins and kisses me again.

My first kiss, and my second kiss, were way better than I imagined. Soft lips, not-stinky breath, and someone I really like.

Then I take his hand and lead him out of the pop-up and into the sun.

"We've got a party to go to," I say. "Let's get pretzels."

Chapter 22

One week after our triumphant home meet, the Eels swim their hearts out at the all-league championship meet. Our stellar performance clinches the league title, despite the earlier loss against Maple Grove.

I can still hear the cheers from our postseason awards night as I sit on the pool deck with my sketchbook on a Wednesday evening. Swim team season is over, and school starts next week. The sky is a cotton candy pink, and the lights come on earlier than they did at the beginning of summer. It's still hot during the day, but I bring a sweatshirt in my bag for after dark.

Ez started preseason practice at Tomlin this week, so she's been busy every afternoon. Busy, but happy. I get texts from her every night full of smiley faces. Tonight, Nico texted that he's going to the store for school supplies with Owen and Aidan, but that they might come by the pool when they're done. I keep watching the gate, hoping to see a tall, dark-haired boy walk through it.

While I still have light, I work on the sketch I started a few weeks ago—the one that shows the pool layout like a blueprint. But I'm not working on it for the same reason I was before—to help me figure out how someone could cause a chlorine leak. Now I'm working on it because I want to remember the East Valley pool exactly like it is now.

Because it's about to change.

Across the pool, Dad stands between the locker rooms and the chlorine tanks, pointing and talking excitedly while two contractors measure distances and take notes. Work will begin on the new chlorination system next week when we all go back to school. Locker room renovations begin after that. They're even talking about expanding the Snack Shack and getting new blocks and lane lines. It's all good changes, but it's lots of changes.

The construction guys aren't the only ones working. Charlotte bustles behind the Snack Shack counter, baseball hat covering her hair, selling hot dogs and pretzels with a legitimate smile on her face. Mom and Dad made a deal with her that she would work at the pool every day for the rest of the summer and they wouldn't press charges on her for causing the chlorine leak and vandalizing the pool.

The thing is, I've never seen Charlotte happier. Just as I'm shading in the blocks in my sketch, Charlotte takes a break to bring me a pretzel.

"Maddie!" She bounces. "Did you get your schedule? Do we have any classes together?"

I tuck my sketchbook in my bag and pull out my phone to show her my class schedule. She grabs it from me and scrutinizes the list. "Ooh! History, third period! That's what I have too."

"Awesome." I smile.

"But that's it." She hands me back my phone. "You're doing art for your elective again, huh?"

I nod. "What's your elective?"

"Drama." She flips her hair, and I stifle a giggle. "I know. You can laugh. It's completely appropriate. But I'm pretty excited about it."

"Your parents are letting you do theater?"

"Not exactly." Charlotte rolls her eyes. "My parents are letting me do drama as an elective for eighth grade, and I have to work here and get good grades, and then maybe I can do a real play at a real theater."

"That seems generous for your parents. They're not mad that you decided to stop swimming?"

"Um, no, they're definitely mad. But I think they also feel kind of guilty about the whole mess, so . . ."

"And you don't miss swimming?" I feel like I know the answer.

"Not yet. I thought I would, but honestly I haven't really enjoyed swimming in years." Charlotte sighs. "I liked it when I won things, obviously, but the burnout is real."

"I can see that," I say. "So, how's work? Gets hot in the Shack sometimes, huh?"

"It's not so bad," she says. And it can't be, since she hasn't stopped smiling since she sat down. "It's way better than juvenile hall or picking up trash on the side of the road, or whatever else I probably should be doing." Her smile fades a little.

"Plus, free Popsicles," I say, to bring the smile back.

It works. "Yep!" Charlotte grins. "Plus, the lifeguard is kind of hot."

"Ew, no! That's my brother!" I punch her in the arm, and she yelps, which draws Jack's attention on the lifeguard stand. He blows his whistle.

"No fighting on the pool deck!" he hollers, but he's laughing as he says it.

Charlotte puts her hands sweetly under her chin and bats her eyelashes at him.

"Ah! Stop flirting with my brother!" I whisper-yell, and Charlotte and I dissolve into giggles.

We're still giggling as Ez walks in the pool gate, sporting a new cow-print bucket hat.

"Hey!" I holler and wave. "Cute hat. I thought you weren't coming because you had practice at Tomlin?"

"We got done early." Ez smiles and plops onto the chaise lounge next to me. "What's so funny?"

"Ugh, Charlotte thinks my brother is hot." I roll my eyes.

Ez laughs. "Everyone thinks your brother is hot."

Charlotte shrugs. "I didn't say I'm trying to date him! I'm just saying he's nice to look at." Then she gets serious. "Speaking of inappropriate crushes, what's going to happen with Lucas?"

"Good question! So, it turns out he actually shoplifted the eggs he threw at our pool, and the snow globe."

"What?" Charlotte yells. "He gave you a present that he *stole*? Oh my god, what a loser."

I smile and go on. "Yeah, anyway, his parents are super pissed. But they're also divorcing. He didn't just tell me that to make me feel sorry for him. When my mom called the school to tell them to keep us out of the same classes, they said he wasn't enrolled. Apparently, the school secretary is pretty chatty. I guess his mom wants to start over in a new town at a different school. He is moving far, far away."

"Good, 'cause we have way better boys to think about." Ez glances at the gate, where Owen, Aidan, and Nico walk in wearing their backpacks. They're grinning and talking loudly, lightly sweaty from bike riding. My stomach buzzes when Nico spots me.

Aidan climbs over my chaise lounge before sitting on Ez's. He takes his backpack off and zips it open. "Hey, Friend Zone! You will not believe how awesome our school supplies are. Check out these gel pens!" He holds up a box.

"Ooh, I love gel pens," I say as I scoot forward in my chaise, just enough to allow Nico to sit behind me so I can lean against him.

"Hi," he says, bending his knees so I can sit against his legs. This is a thing we do now—sit right up close together.

I turn and look into his dark eyes. My face grows warm. "Hi."

"I had a feeling you liked gel pens," he says, and

reaches into his pocket to present me with a packaged light-blue gel pen.

"Oh! I love it!" I turn over the package. "Thank you."

Owen tosses a random school supply at us. I think it's an eraser. "You two are obnoxiously adorable, you know that, right?"

"I know." Nico grins and looks at me again. "But the color just made me think of you because it was, like, pool-water color."

Aidan squeezes Nico's shoulder. "Maddie's not the only swimmer who swims in light-blue pools, you know."

"But she's the only swimmer I thought of when I saw the pen," Nico says.

Aidan sighs dreamily. "You two are adorable. I love it. But this is still a friend zone. Just because you two kiss sometimes doesn't mean we're not all still friends, and last time I checked, this is still a zone."

"Obviously." I giggle and throw the eraser back at Owen.

Owen catches it and sits on the end of the chaise lounge Charlotte occupies. "Fine, fine, you two are cute, and we're not at all jealous, because this here is a friend zone." He turns to Charlotte. "So, do we get pretzels from you now or is it still Maddie? This is still a food zone, too, right?"

"Oh!" Charlotte hops up. "I have to get back to work! And no, you have to pay for your pretzels. No freebies. The East Valley pool is a very serious business." She wags a finger at him.

Owen looks wounded. "She's tough."

I smile as Charlotte hurries down the pool deck to the Snack Shack. "She's trying to make up for everything. It's kind of impressive."

Ez smiles. "Yeah, it is. And it turns out working the Snack Shack makes her a lot happier than chasing a black line on the bottom of the pool."

I reach out and grab my best friend's hand. "Not you though."

"Nope, not me." She squeezes my hand. "Chasing a black line is my life."

Aidan leans over and grabs both our hands. "I want to hold hands too!" Everyone laughs.

"What a weird summer," Owen says as he gets comfortable on the chaise lounge Charlotte vacated.

Ez hoots, "You're telling me! But after the chlorine poisoning wore off, it turned out to be a pretty great summer after all."

"Even with all the hunting for clues and looking for mysterious pool vandals?" I whisper.

Ez smiles. "Especially with all that." She leans back in her chaise and folds her hands behind her head. "I got the scholarship I wanted, we won the league, and we finally got Lucas Bryce to leave you alone. Perfect."

"Agreed," I reply. Across the pool, Charlotte closes up the Snack Shack window for the night, and Jack hangs up his lifeguard whistle. I glance back at Nico, who's laughing at something Aidan said.

Then I look at my best friend and feel a smile spread across my face. "Best summer ever."

Acknowledgments

First thanks goes to my mom: my first reader in everything I write and my first champion. Thank you for your unending support and unconditional love. Thanks to my dad, who would be just as proud of this book as he was when I swam the 100-yard butterfly. To my brother, David, thank you for being the best and bravest lifeguard in town. You are my hero.

Thank you to my agent, Melissa Edwards, for your incredible wisdom, your hard work, and for championing feminist middle grade stories. Thanks also to Madelyn Burt and the team at Stonesong.

To Mari Kesselring, I am so grateful for the way you completely understood Maddie's story and brought it into the world. To Meg Gaertner, thank you for taking on this book with excitement and grace. Thanks also to Emily Temple, Taylor Kohn, Heather McDonough, Jackie Dever, Sarah Taplin, and everyone at Jolly Fish Press. Special thanks to Carl Pearce for bringing Maddie to life on this beautiful cover.

I don't know what stroke of fate or luck sat me at a table with Lisa Schmid and Carol Adler at that SCBWI conference in 2016, but I am forever grateful to have you as my friends and critique partners. Thank you to my SCBWI friends, readers, and CPs past and present:

Lou Ann Barnett, Sally Lotz, Joanna Rowland, and Jenny Lundquist.

To my agent sibs, it brings me such happiness to be part of such a supportive and interesting group! Thank you to Sierra Godfrey, who gave me such great insight on alopecia, and to Brigit Young, Bridget Farr, and Julia Nobel for reading and supporting this book.

Thank you to Jessie Lee for choosing me and helping me on this path, and to Carly Heath for the continued support of my writing journey. Thank you to Jaclyn Montano for making me feel comfortable while making me look good, and to Shauna McGuinness for the blog feature and support.

Thank you to Mr. Robert Shibley at Leigh High School, who told me I was a writer, and to Dr. Monza Naff at the University of Oregon, who told me I was a feminist. I'm so grateful to teachers who recognized my interests and skills.

Thanks to the Montevideo Piranhas for being the cornerstone of my childhood summers and the Fulton-El Camino Stingrays for bringing swim team back into my life just in time for this book. Thanks especially to Miriam, the best swim team friend I could ask for.

Thank you to my dear friends Roxana and Bryan Cheah, who built my website and constantly support my family; to Emilie Barnes, who hosts the best front-porch celebrations; to the Tomlin family for the use of your academic-sounding name; and to my playgroup and neighborhood friends, whose support never ends. To my "Until We're Little Old Ladies" book club: Emily, Jennifer, Kristen, Laura, and Susan, thank you for keeping me engaged in books and reading through the years. I'm not sure I would have considered writing books without you.

To my extended family, thank you for all the likes, the shares, the retweets, and the unending support. Thank you to Mamie and Fred; Papa and Bubbie; Jeannie, Chris, and Ava; David, Jessica, and Auggie; and all my amazing aunts, uncles, and cousins. Special thanks to my aunt Mary and the ladies in the kayak crew. Your support of my writing gives me such joy.

To my fiery Isabel, thank you for filling my life with curiosity and laughter. To my sweet Lilly, thank you for loving books with me.

And to my husband, thank you for the incredible support of this dream, which for several years brought more frustration than joy. The best times are ahead of us.

About the Author

Catherine Arguelles has worked as a counselor with middle school students, a fundraiser for nonprofit organizations, and a volunteer at schools and libraries. She is the proud parent of two feminist readers and three regal cats. Catherine lives in Northern California, and her favorite event was once the 100-yard backstroke.